AN HONEST BETRAYAL

AN HONEST
BETRAYAL

Jeffrey Ashford

This first world edition published in Great Britain 1999 by
SEVERN HOUSE PUBLISHERS LTD of
9–15 High Street, Sutton, Surrey SM1 1DF.
This first world edition published in the U.S.A. 1999 by
SEVERN HOUSE PUBLISHERS INC of
595 Madison Avenue, New York, N.Y. 10022.

British Library Cataloguing in Publication Data
Ashford, Jeffrey, 1926-
    An honest betrayal
    1.   Detective and mystery stories
    I.   Title
    823.9'14 [F]

    ISBN 0-7278-5459-3

All situations in this publication are fictitious and
any resemblance to living persons is purely coincidental.

Typeset by Palimpsest Book Production Ltd.,
Polmont, Stirlingshire, Scotland.
Printed and bound in Great Britain by
MPG Books Ltd, Bodmin, Cornwall.

One

He had been christened Neal Albert, but called himself John; Doe had an odd sense of humour.

"That's it," Osman said, as he braked the car to a halt.

Doe looked down the sloping land at the distant Victorian house surrounded by garden and fields. Two floors high and L-shaped, the wing was almost as large as the main part; on one side was a walled garden, on the other, a swimming pool. Beyond the pool was a tall yew hedge, then a fifty-acre field which rose up to a small copse of mixed wood that had not been coppiced for many years. "Where's the nearest road that way?" He pointed.

"Three, four hundred yards. No problem."

An ignorant assessment. A stranger crossing a field immediately drew the attention of anyone in sight of him; on top of that, at a distance, it was impossible to judge whether the ground offered any unusual obstacles.

"And there he goes!"

Doe looked back. Two men, their figures slightly foreshortened because of the angle at which they were being viewed, walked past the corner of the pool to the poolhouse, into which they disappeared.

"You want glasses?" Without waiting for an answer, or warning what he was going to do, Osman roughly reached past Doe and opened the glove compartment, brought out a leather binocular case. "Here. Watch the loving couple."

"Better not. With the sun where it is, it could reflect on the glasses and someone down there might note the flashes. I can see all I need without 'em."

"Suit yourself." He again reached across and jammed the case back into the glove compartment, resentful at being corrected.

"Let's move," Doe said. "We've been stopped long enough; we don't want to catch their attention."

"You reckon there's anyone down there that sharp?"

"Could be."

"They could be angels, but they ain't." Osman started the engine and as he released the handbrake, another car crested the hill behind them. Common sense, let alone courtesy, should have caused him to wait to let the other car pass; common sense and courtesy had never been his strengths. He drew out and accelerated.

The oncoming driver, having to brake, hooted his displeasure.

"Take your bleeding L-plates off," Osman shouted into the wind.

Doe decided to tell Cairns that he didn't want Osman on the actual job. He would need a back-up who could be relied upon, not one who flaunted a ridiculous machismo. "I want to go through Childerton," he said, in his low, soft voice.

"Why?"

"To look at things. D'you know Frewer Street?"

"No."

He unclipped his seat belt – Osman had jeered at him for using it – and turned round to reach over for the small guide pamphlet on the back seat. The car swerved sharply, throwing him against the door pillar.

"Bloody dog," Osman said.

Doe regained his balance, picked up the pamphlet, settled back and clipped the belt home. He was certain there'd been no dog – had there been, Osman would have enjoyed running it over. That swerve had signalled a moronic sense of humour. He opened the pamphlet at the middle and studied the street plan of central Childerton. "When we get there, we want to go down to the bottom of the High Street to a T-junction, and then take the left-hand road. Giulio is on the right-hand side."

"What's that when it's at home?"

"An Italian restaurant."

"Wop food is crap."

"It's certainly different from fish and chips."

"What's that supposed to mean?"

"That taste is a personal matter . . . According to this, if we carry on to the end of that road and turn right, we'll come to a car park."

"Any more bleeding orders?"

"Not for the moment."

Osman mumbled something, his tone angry, but the words unintelligible.

Doe enjoyed an inward smile. It was gratifying to be certain that the other had been careful not to be understood. Osman viewed him with scorn, yet that scorn was edged with uneasiness, perhaps even a twitch of fear.

As they drove past fields, some harvested or still with standing corn, some carrying farm animals, Osman's antagonistic yet uneasy attitude prompted in Doe's mind a series of brief memories. The misery of a childhood in which he had been the victim of every bully; his inability, in his teens, to enjoy friendships; the unexpected discovery that he was a naturally gifted shot with both rifle and handgun (and had that aroused resentment among several shots who had valued their skills too highly!); the circumstances leading to his employing his gift profitably; the first time he'd killed; the first time he'd enjoyed the reluctant respect that his skill garnered; the passion he'd been able to buy . . .

They entered Childerton from the north and passed through an area of small terraced houses built at the turn of the century to house the labour force brought in to work the then newly established factories. Further on, they passed a large garage, went over a railway bridge, and came up to a line of cars waiting to go forward past some road works. As he stopped, Osman cursed the delay; when the cars ahead began to move only slowly, he hooted to try to hurry them up. As they came level with the man directing the traffic, the other shouted: "Keep your knickers on, mate."

"You reckon I'd take 'em off for the likes of you?" Osman laughed at his own 'wit'.

Doe suffered an unwelcome uncertainty. If Cairns was smart, would he have given Osman the job of handling this first reconnaissance? Wouldn't he have found someone with more self-control? It was a question to remember.

The High Street, originally a very wide road, had been narrowed by the provision of a bus and unloading lane. Once, the shops lining it had been small and family owned, mostly offering quality and service; now, with few exceptions, these had been replaced by multi-stores which provided cheapness rather than quality and ignored service.

"At the bottom of the road, take the left-hand turn," Doe said.

"I heard you before."

That was no guarantee of anything.

The traffic was thick and it took them time to move along the road; as Doe listened to Osman's swearing, he wondered why a language with so rich a vocabulary should suffer such small variety in swear words.

They turned left into a much narrower one-way road; halfway along was a double bow-fronted building above the front door of which, in very modest gold lettering, was the name 'Giulio' – nothing to indicate that this was a restaurant.

Such modesty, Doe thought, meant upmarket prices and a maître d' who could identify a pleb even when wearing a suit from Anderson and Shepherd.

"Where's this place you was wanting?" Osman asked.

"It's on your right now."

He turned to look. "You don't catch me eating in a joint like that."

The maître d' would be grateful to hear that.

They reached a crossroads and a parking sign directed them to turn right; a couple of hundred yards on was a municipal car park.

Doe released his safety belt. "I don't know how long I'll be."

"I'm not a bloody chaffeur."

"No sweat. If you're gone by the time I'm back, I'll give Dave a ring and ask him to send someone else along to pick me up."

Osman, certain what Cairns's reaction would be to such a message, swore yet again.

Doe left the car and walked back to the crossroads, then slowly along Frewer Street on the opposite side to Giulio. He had an exceptional memory and later would be able to 'play back' the scene in his mind and recall all relevant details.

In the High Street he went into a newsagent and asked for a copy of the *Daily Telegraph*; none was available and he was offered *The Times*. He refused to buy this – his mother had always maintained that his father was an Australian who'd deserted her in 'her hour of need'. He had often wondered why she'd singled out this one man. He returned to Frewer Street and walked back on the opposite side. As he drew level with Giulio, he checked the building opposite – from the window on the top floor, there hung a notice advertising a spacious office to rent; a slice of luck.

By turning left and left again, he entered a road that ran

parallel with Frewer Street. Backing the building in which was the office to let was a small private car park, which could be reached through a narrow passage that ran between an estate agent and an electrical store. Access to the office couldn't have been easier.

Shoreland was many miles from any shore; tradition suggested its name was a corruption of Shareland, a possibility rejected by cynics on the grounds that even in medieval times no local had ever willingly shared anything. Notable for its many black and white buildings and for the ruins of St Augustine's Abbey, which had once possessed a thigh bone of the saint, it had a character that not even a succession of local planning officers had succeeded in destroying.

In the end bedroom on the second floor of the Dolphin and Anchor Hotel, Doe went through to the small en suite bathroom and examined his nose in the mirror; the pimple was not yet ripe for popping. He fussed over his appearance, ignoring the fact that nothing would overcome the disadvantages of thinning hair, narrow forehead, watery pale blue eyes, button nose, weak mouth, hardly discernible chin, and slack body.

He returned to the bedroom, checked the door was locked, brought out of the cupboard one of the two matching oblong leather cases and put this on the bed. On the lid were the initials 'S.P.T.' in large gold lettering. He was certain S.P.T. had been old fashioned, archetypal upper-class – insultingly superior or condescendingly polite, using wealth to bully his way through life. He undid the two straps, unlocked and opened the lid. He ran the tips of his fingers along the beautifully grained stock until they reached the butt. Only a female butt could provide an equal tactile pleasure.

He brought the 26″ fully ribbed barrels and stock out of the case, locked them together, snapped the fore-end home.

An Honest Betrayal

He put the 8lb sporting rifle to his shoulder and aimed it at an imaginary man, his forefinger caressing the for'd trigger. Gentle pressure and the heavy .450 bullet would shatter the man's head . . .

Two

Two hundred and thirty-five miles to the south, Ballard walked into Detective Sergeant Frost's room on the fourth floor of the nine-floor divisional HQ. "I'm back, Sarge."

"I'd never have guessed if you hadn't told me," Frost said drily, his voice deep and husky. "So what's the result?"

"Mrs Segal doesn't want to press charges. She now says her boyfriend didn't really mean it . . . I don't understand. She looks like she's been in a ten-round heavyweight contest, yet says it was just a misunderstanding. What's more, it's only a few weeks from last time. Why does she put up with it?"

Frost opened the top drawer of his desk and brought out a pouch of tobacco and a packet of papers, rolled a thin cigarette. "Love, hope, fear, resignation, who knows except her and maybe she doesn't. Still, she's saved us a bundle of paperwork." He lit the cigarette.

"I tried to persuade her for her own sake to press charges."

"That was a fool thing to do."

"But one day he's going to take things too far and kill her."

"Listen. Someone gets knocked down and complains, it's our job to find out who did the knocking, not to pick 'em up and dust 'em down when they say they just tripped."

"But . . ."

"How long have you been active?"

"Three years."

8

"Then it's time enough to have learned some common sense."

Ballard was silent. The detective sergeant was set in his opinions.

"Did you drop the papers at the Guv'nor's place?"

"He wasn't there, but his wife said she'll give them to him as soon as he returns."

"He wasn't back from county HQ? That'll fire up his temper. Spread the word to double-check all reports before they're handed in." Frost stubbed out the cigarette, which had quickly burned down.

"Mrs Lock seems a very pleasant woman."

"Sure."

"More friendly than some of the other wives of senior officers I've met. She offered me coffee."

"Which, being on duty, you refused?"

Ballard said humorously: "I thought of doing so, but decided it might have seemed rude to turn the offer down."

"You've some queer ideas. Comes from too much learning."

Frost was forever decrying the worth of academic, as opposed to experiential, learning; his constant denigration suggested he was conscious of his own restricted education.

"So you wasted an hour drinking coffee and eating iced cakes?"

"One cup of coffee, one chocolate biscuit, and I was out inside a quarter of an hour."

Frost rolled another cigarette.

"I suppose she gets a bit lonely with the Guv'nor working all hours and no kids."

"Why should she complain when life's so generous?"

Frost's view of children was well known. "She's quite something to look at. I've been told she was into modelling before she married him."

9

"Maybe."

"You don't know?"

"Not interested."

"There's a bit of talk about her, isn't there?"

"Is there?"

"One of the lads was saying he had to call when the Guv'nor wasn't around and she was giving signals."

"What the hell are you talking about?"

"Well, you know."

"I wouldn't bloody ask if I did."

"He reckoned . . . If he'd made a move, it wouldn't have been rank she pulled."

"Your mate needs his mind scrubbed with Dettol." Frost leaned back in his chair, the unlit cigarette in his hand. "D'you think it smart to repeat that sort of talk?"

"No, but . . ."

"Then why do it?"

Ballard was silent.

"Haven't you anything to do but repeat someone else's filth?"

He left the room. If Mrs Lock had been just an ordinary wife, Frost would probably have shown lubricious interest in the possibility; because she was his senior officer's wife, he viewed the idea as blasphemy. Of the old school, he believed in the benefits of hard policing, still bemoaned the rescinding of the sus laws, held the Police Code of Discipline in contempt, and blamed PACE – the Police and Criminal Evidence Act – for the ever-increasing incidence of crime.

The only occupant of the CID general room was Turner. Ballard walked past the noticeboard, plastered with so many notices and photographs calling for identification of individuals that they were ignored, stepped around a canvas holdall that should have been taken down to the property room, and

sat at his desk which, since he was not even a full member of
CID, was in the draughtiest corner.

"Where have you been skiving?" Turner asked.

"Playing two-up with a bunch of Aussies and beating 'em
hollow."

"You're a lying bastard. We can't even beat 'em at tiddly-
winks . . . Geoff, old boy, I need a couple of tenners worse
than a starving man needs grub."

"So what's new?"

"My whole future's at stake. There's this hot number all
lined up, but she's got ideas beyond her potential. If I give
her the Ritz treatment, she'll quit stalling."

"How long do you want it for?"

"Next pay day. You've no need for it. Your steady gives
you all the essentials and feeds you on top of that."

He wondered how fierce would Turner's scorn be if told that
he and Fleur were limiting their amorous pleasures. "I need
every penny to buy a house and furnish it."

"That's in the future. I need the money now."

He reached into the pocket of his lightweight jacket and
brought out his wallet.

"Tell you what, mate, make it thirty. When you order a
bottle of wine instead of just a glass each, they go weak at
the knees."

He checked the money in his wallet. "I can only make it
twenty-five."

Turner came across and sat on the desk. "Then I'll have
to rely on proven technique to make up the difference." He
held out his hand. "You're helping to make someone the
luckiest young lady this side of nirvana," he said as he took
the money.

"Here's hoping she doesn't end up wishing she'd stayed the
other side . . . Ian told me something the other day."

"Never believe a word he says."

11

"He had to go to the DI's house to leave something and only Mrs Lock was there. According to him, she was giving signals."

"He'd shock anyone."

"He swears she'd have said yes."

"That lad lives in fantasy land."

"That's what I said, more or less, but he swore it was true . . . She wouldn't act like that, would she?"

"Not with him if she's any taste."

"Not with anyone. She is the DI's wife."

"What difference does that make? Are you so stupid you think that because she's married to a senior officer, she wouldn't flash her pants at a plod? Where were you when common sense was being handed out? Killing your brains with learning?"

As did the sergeant, Turner resented the fact that he was a graduate, but for a different reason; his degree put him in the fast lane for promotion.

"Pin your ears back and learn about the real world out there. Women are the same, whether their husbands are dustmen or dukes. They get bored when hubby's away at work, so when a good-looking bloke – which doesn't include Ian – turns up, they start wondering what's below his belt."

"I suppose that could just happen . . ."

"It does, all the time."

"You're just hopeful!"

"Gawd, there's none so blind as those who think marriage is as good as a chastity belt. I'll let you into the secret of the truth. I hadn't been in uniform a fortnight when a burglary that didn't sound much was reported; CID couldn't be bothered, so I was sent along. The door was opened by a reasonable number wearing a short housecoat over a nightdress. She looks at me and my shining new uniform and smiles.'What's been nicked?' I ask, keen to do the job real efficient. 'I don't know,' she answers. 'Then suppose you show me where they forced an entry and after that check what's missing?' She leads me to the downstairs bog and has a bit of a laugh about the burglar having put his foot in it, then goes off to count the silver. There was a window which had had a single pane of frosted glass; chummy had used glue and padding and smashed it. There'd been a couple of other jobs with the same technique so I reckon to get on to CID and tell 'em it's worth getting interested and sending along a SOCO to see what he can find. Then I remember I've left the wife checking and she might be messing up something important, so I hurry into the dining-room. She was bending over, checking the contents of the bottom drawer of the dresser, and what with the nightdress and the housecoat both being short, nothing was in hiding. But instead of jumping up and blushing purple, she stayed as she was and asked if I'd noticed anything interesting . . . It was quite a time before I phoned CID."

"A grave dereliction of duty."

"Sometimes," Turner said, as he slid off the desk to stand, "I wonder if you'll ever get the priorities sorted out."

"I still wonder—" He stopped.

"What?"

"Would someone in Mrs Lock's position really ever behave like that?"

"Why the curiosity? Are you wondering whether to try your luck?"

"When I'm engaged?"

That was the funniest thing Turner had heard for a long while.

Three

Cairns looked like a man who had sampled all the vices and wondered why there were so few. "Give us your glass," he said.

"I haven't quite finished," Doe said.

"You're a man who takes his time."

"It usually pays."

"But never enough!" Cairns laughed.

The door opened and a man in his early twenties, dressed with care and deliberate outrageous taste, came to a halt a pace inside the room. "Oh! I didn't know you had a guest. I'm terribly sorry, David."

"You weren't to know, Ronnie, were you?"

"Is he an important guest?"

"You could say that."

"I don't think I would."

"It's lucky for us that appearances really can be deceptive, isn't it?" Doe said.

"Oh, dear, did I say something to upset you?"

"No offence meant and none taken," Cairns said quickly.

"I hope not. I do so hate upsetting people."

"Sure. Look, this is business."

"And you want to be left alone. Well, I'm sure I don't have to worry about doing that because appearances would have to be completely deceptive." He turned, closed the door behind himself.

14

"He's a great comic," Cairns said.

Doe thought of other descriptions.

Cairns crossed to the large cocktail cabinet, beautifully inlaid and with elaborate hinges, lock surround, and handle, which played part of the drinking song from *The Tales of Hoffmann* when the doors were opened. Schmaltz appealed to him. He poured himself a large measure of Laphroaig and added a little bottled water. Luxury appealed to him. He returned to his chair and sat, slightly out of breath. Rest appealed to him. "So let's have the story."

"It's no good staking out the house."

There was a heavily chased silver cigar box on the occasional table by his side and he opened the lid, brought out a cigar. "D'you use these?"

"I don't smoke."

"You'll end up playing a harp," he said sarcastically. He liked men to act like men – most of the time, that is. "The place is out on its own; there's nothing overlooking it."

"That's the danger."

He lit the cigar with a non-safety match, drew on it, let the smoke trickle out through his hairy nostrils. "What danger?"

"That isolated, anything extra is going to be noticed. After I've shot him, it'll take time to cross the fields and if they're smart enough to move quick, they could head me off. Another thing. There's often a farmhand around in the countryside. I'm not risking an eyewitness."

"If you're that shit-scared of someone behind every hedge, use the woods."

"The copse is maybe a hundred and fifty feet above the house. A longish downward shot, especially if there's a wind to create eddies, can become too tricky to be certain."

Cairns jabbed the air with his cigar. "You're sounding like you're getting ready to quit. What's the real problem? You're not half as good as you think because there's a yellow streak from your belly to your back?"

"Where's the nearest phone?"

"Why?"

"I'll ring Ed and tell him you've no confidence in me so he needs to find someone else."

Cairns went to speak, checked the words, picked up his glass and drained it. He put the cigar down on an ashtray, stood, took his glass across to the cocktail cabinet and poured himself another large whisky to the accompaniment of the drinking song. "Can't you take a bit of fun? Christ! I'm not saying you ain't so good you're in a league of your own."

Doe inwardly laughed. He'd forced the other to eat crow!

Cairns returned to his chair and sat, drank, picked up the cigar and drew on it. "So what's the form?"

"I remembered you telling me Bob's gone legit with an Italian restaurant in Childerton and eats there most nights. I told Jack to drive me to see it."

"And?"

"On the opposite side of the road is an office to let. It'll be empty and at night-time there'll be good street lighting; at such short range, it doesn't signify it'll be a downward shot."

In his surprise, Cairns spoke loudly. "You'll raise the bloody town."

"One shot. People who can't see what's happening will think it's a car backfiring, people who can will be panicking. The office building backs on to a small private car park with access to the next road so a smart getaway is made. It'll need someone to force an entry to the office. There's bound to be some security."

"A crappy alarm system. One of the boys'll have that silent within thirty seconds."

"There are two points to make clear. I don't want Jack with me."

16

"Why not?"

"He's a loud-mouthed fool."

"You're quick to complain."

"When necessary."

"What else?"

"I want a woman ready for when it's finished. And she's got to be class, not a scrubber."

"The orders are to take you straight down to the coast . . ."

"I always have a woman afterwards." He was silent for a couple of seconds, then said: "It's never so good at other times."

Cairns was almost shocked at the thought that someone should enjoy added pleasure because he had murdered.

Four

The county force had abolished section houses many years before and, to compensate for the lack of subsidised housing, had introduced a rent allowance; this, when interest rates were reasonable, helped to meet the repayments of most mortgages.

Ballard lived in a flat above a newsagent in eastern Staple Cross; very small, with unusually shaped rooms because the building stood at the corner of two roads which converged at an acute angle, it had the advantage of a rent sufficiently low for him to be able to add generously to his savings each month: savings that would meet the deposit when he bought a house.

Marriage could not come quickly enough. Fleur was clad in the beauty of a thousand stars. And if it were whispered that her features possessed slight irregularities, he would very quickly point out that these spelled character. She kept her hair, which had a natural wave, short whatever the prevailing fashion. Her dark brown eyes were so lustrous they could have charmed the truth even out of a politician. Her lips were shaped for passion. To call her neck swanlike was to flatter swans. She was slim, not catwalk skinny, and her curves curved as curves should . . .

Her parents were out and they were spending the evening at her home; dinner had been cooked by her. "Is it all right?" she asked.

"Delicious," he answered immediately.

"You're not just saying that? You don't think it maybe needed a little more cooking? The apples are still crunchy."

"Which is exactly how I like them."

"I must make a mental note, cooked apples to be crunchy . . . Isn't it fun finding out things about each other? Is there something you particularly like that I don't know about?"

"Yes."

She laughed; when she laughed, humour captured her whole face. "I said, that I don't know about." She reached across the table to put a hand on his. "Darling, you do really agree it's better to wait, don't you? It'll make marriage so very special."

And unique, he thought. She was, at the same time, of the present and of the past; brought up to respect standards that were now seldom observed.

She withdrew her hand after a quick squeeze. "Would you like some cheese?"

"After such a feast? Impossible!"

"Then Father said to offer you port. He's just bought a few bottles with unexpected money from shares."

"You're pushing the boat right out!"

"He is, I'm not, especially as it's so special he's like a miser with it. You're very honoured."

"I kowtow in respectful gratitude. Are you going to have some?"

"I don't like it."

"Then it would be a complete waste on me because I haven't had enough to know the good from the bad."

"So we'll leave it all to him to sniff and declaim over. Let's go through to the sitting room."

"What about clearing the table?"

"I'll do that after you've gone."

"You sound as if you're expecting me to leave early."

"You're not staying late because you look tired and I'm sure you need a good night's sleep." She saw he was about to speak. "No argument. You leave at half-past ten."

"Or my car will turn into a pumpkin?"

They went through the kitchen to the hall, triangular in shape because of the outshut, and from there into the sitting room, which was more heavily beamed than the other rooms and had a large inglenook fireplace. "You sit there and I'll sit here," she said.

"I've a more friendly suggestion."

"I'm sure you have." She spoke with mock seriousness. "But one should always rest after a meal."

"Why is good advice always boring?" He sat where she'd indicated. Before he left, he'd persuade her that their meals had settled . . .

"Darling, is something troubling you?" she asked as she studied him.

"What makes you ask?"

"Before supper you spent quite a long time just staring into space and now you're doing the same thing. What are you thinking about?"

It seemed tactful to say: "Just mental rambling."

"You're sure nothing's gone wrong at work?"

"Not as far as I'm concerned. The sarge has been bellyaching, but that's his character."

"Father was asking me when you're likely to gain promotion. I said in two to three years. Was that right?"

Her parents, he could be certain, were hoping it was. They liked him, but would have preferred him to have a higher profile in life to match their own background; class had been abolished by the politicians, long live class. "Three at the most, provided I don't make a right B.U. of something." He'd joined the county force under the Special Entry Scheme; this meant he did two years on the beat to complete initial training and probation, three to four more years in different departments to gain further experience, and then could expect special training and accelerated promotion to inspector. The scheme was designed to attract graduates; it gained the resentment of any non-graduates, especially the old hands.

"But we're not waiting until you're an inspector?"

"No way."

"I meant, before we marry," she said with a coquettish smile.

"What else?" He drifted into silence.

"Now where are you? Or shouldn't I ask?"

"I've remembered what I was thinking when you said I went mental walkabout before supper. Sam was going on about how a lot of wives become so bored that if a policeman in uniform turns up during the day when their husbands are out at work, they'll give him the old come-on."

"How very typical! Does he ever think about anything but sex?"

"I've heard him discuss football once or twice."

"He needs to see a psychiatrist."

"Be fair, it's probably more hope than experience. And in this instance, I started the discussion."

"How?"

"I mentioned Ian had said that when he'd called at the DI's house to give him something, but he was out, Mrs Lock gave the impression that if he'd like some fun, she was in a humorous mood."

"Some of your colleagues are sick."

"Felix agrees with that sentiment!"

"You're not saying you repeated to him what Ian said?"

He tried to answer without lying and hesitated too long.

"What a beastly thing to do! You know the idea to be absurd and it's throughly demeaning to repeat it. Why did you?" She didn't pause for an answer. "You've always said the force is a macho society, so I suppose this sort of nastiness is considered amusing. You were trying to be one of the boys."

"Hang on . . ."

"That you could suggest Mrs Lock isn't a loving wife! Or do you think that loving wives ask strangers up to their bedrooms because they're bored?"

"Of course I don't . . ."

"I suppose that when we're married you're going to spend your time at work wondering what I'm up to."

"How can you suggest . . ."

"Could I be asking the milkman up for a quickie?"

"You know that's ridiculous . . ."

"Do I? Maybe you're always secretly hoping a door will be opened by a bored wife with gleaming eyes? And what will you tell me when you finally return home? That you've had an exhausting day?"

There were times when the course of a woman's mind resembled that of the Hooghly River. He hurriedly stood, crossed to the settee and sat by her side, apologised for his stupidity and assured her that if Venus opened the door to him, he'd turn his back on her until she'd dressed. He was glad that earlier he hadn't explained how it had been the attitude of the detective inspector's wife which had intrigued him and made him wonder if . . .

Five

The phone in Doe's room rang. He put down the paperback and crossed to the bedside table, lifted the receiver.

"Half an hour." The line went dead.

Jenner would be dining at Giulio. Information bought from someone in his mob. Cynics said that everyone could be bought, but that wasn't true. When he contracted to do a job, he would do it exactly as promised, even if offered a fortune not to. A man must honour himself.

He returned to the armchair and let his mind probe the future. Afterwards, he would be driven to a motel and there a woman would be waiting. He would prove an Atlas in love. If only he could always enjoy such success. Yet however much he tried at other times, he could never match the strength he enjoyed immediately after a successful job . . .

He returned to the present. He put the gun case on the bed, undid the straps, opened the lid. He ran his fingers along the stock, then the barrels. This rifle proved both the truth and the falsity of the proposition that all men were equal.

It could kill any man, but not every man could successfully use it to kill. Even when shooting at a target, nerves played a large part in deciding if one was a good, moderate, or poor shot; when the target was human and breathed and moved, nerves could make a mind shiver and hands tremble until the sights performed a jig. Yet his mind laughed, his hands became locked, the sights motionless . . .

23

He closed and locked the lid, secured the straps. He packed his clothes in the second case, which was a facsimile of the first – seeing the two together, there would be no suggestion, despite their shape, of a gun case (except perhaps to someone who shot where game was so plentiful that a pair of guns was necessary). The thoughtful man thought of every possibility.

Downstairs, the woman behind the reception desk, tired beyond her age by an invalid husband, couldn't be bothered even to offer him a professional smile. He put the room-locking card on the desk. "I've just had a sudden change of plan and need to leave now, so I'd like my bill, please."

She said wearily: "Guests are requested to give at least one hour's notice of departure, but I'll ask accounts to be as quick as possible."

"Thank you very much."

She turned and went into the small office. He crossed to one of the chairs and sat. As she reappeared, a distinguished-looking man accompanied by a smartly dressed woman who held a coloured lead attached to a chihuahua, went up to the desk. She made a far greater effort to be bright and cheerful . . .

Life was about perceived values, Doe thought, yet those that really shaped lives were the hidden ones. In his mind, he lined cross-wires on the back of the smartly dressed woman's head and rested his finger on the trigger. Squeeze the trigger as gently as a woman's tits, was the usual advice; it had to be done far more delicately than that . . .

Five minutes later, he was called to the reception desk and the receptionist presented him with the bill. "What card?" she asked.

"I'm paying in cash."

Having settled the bill and received the receipt, he checked the time, returned to the chair and sat, a case on either side of his legs. Exactly on the half-hour, he picked up the cases, crossed the foyer to the revolving door, went outside.

"A nice day, sir," said the doorman, dressed in Ruritanian uniform. "You'll be wanting a taxi?"

"No, thanks."

The doorman lost interest and turned away.

A Jaguar drew up. Rayner couldn't be bothered to get out of the car and open the boot for him. He loaded the two cases, closed the boot lid, opened the nearside rear door and climbed in.

"Think you're the bloody boss, sitting in the back?" was Rayner's greeting.

By the end of the day, Doe thought, he'd have proved himself stronger than any boss.

The Jaguar had been stolen the previous day; false number plates had been fitted and the car driven down the hundred miles to Harmsworthy before the owner was aware that it was missing.

They went down the High Street and then round to Ashley Road. "We're in luck," Rayner muttered, his voice pitched slightly higher than normal. There were several free parking bays and one was immediately past the passage leading into the small private car park. He drove smoothly into this.

There were few pedestrians and little traffic – there were no restaurants, cafés, or late-closing shops along the road and it didn't offer a short cut. It was easy to check that there was no cause for alarm.

"Let's move," Doe said, pleasingly certain that McCleary, even if he would never acknowledge it, was reluctant to leave the security of the car. He opened the door and stepped out onto the pavement, reached in for the case, shut the door harder than was necessary, childishly hoping the loud and unnecessary noise would make both of them curse him.

He walked up the passage, followed by McCleary, and into the empty car park. He put the case down, brought a pair of surgical gloves out of his pocket and put these on. McCleary did the same as he visually checked the windows which overlooked the area. "OK," he muttered.

To watch him at work was to watch an artist. He removed the putty around the lowest pane in one of the ground-floor windows, made certain there was no sensory alarm attached directly to the glass before he eased that free. A check with a small probe which was rather like an endoscope showed him where the window frame was wired to the alarm system. Having identified this as both an open and a closed circuit, he used a compass to show which wires carried current, then cut those that didn't and cross-contacted those that did. He opened the window.

Using a torch whose beam was reduced by an adjustable shutter, they made their way along a passage and up three flights of stairs. McCleary forced the lock of the office door almost as quickly as if he had a key.

There were four rooms, the largest of which faced the restaurant. McCleary checked the double window for an alarm. "It's clear."

Doe swung back the inner glass, undid the central catch of the traditional sash window and lowered the upper half until there was a sufficient gap. As he'd expected, street lighting was good. He judged the entrance door of the restaurant to be forty-five feet away; at any much greater distance, he would have used a laser rangefinder to check because accuracy was essential as distance increased. He watched a scrap of paper on the far pavement move along an inch and then stop; move again to come up against the front of an antiques shop. Outside the town there was a light south-westerly wind; buildings could distort direction and even create strong eddies, but the lackadaisical movement of the paper indicated there was no need to make an allowance for wind.

He removed his right-hand glove and put it in his pocket, opened the case and took out the three parts of the rifle, then secured them together. He removed two rounds from the cartridge holder and polished these with a piece of shammy leather even though there was no point to this; it had become a good-luck action. An intelligent man accepted that all the planning in the world could be set to naught by one moment of bad luck. The bullets were a modern version of the dumdum, and after hitting a human body they fragmented to cause tissue and bone destruction out of all proportion to their size. He closed the gun with a metallic snap that caused McCleary to draw in his breath with a sharp hiss. He smiled contemptuously. He left the safety catch on. Perhaps a needless precaution for a man as experienced and skilled as he – the fraction of a second needed to slide it forward might just mean failure – but he was a stickler for good weapon security.

With no way of knowing or judging how long Jenner would stay in the restaurant, they had taken up position early on. After a while, Doe heard sounds of fidgeting. McCleary was becoming more nervous. Waiting sorted out the real men. Soon the other would have to empty his bladder. It would be long after it was all over before he suffered such a need.

The clock of the nearby parish church – graceful seventeenth century, heavy nineteenth century restorations – struck the half-hour. He wondered what Jenner was having for his last meal.

Through the glass front door of the restaurant a pair of legs became visible. He knew these belonged to Jenner; hunters developed an instinct that told them their prey was approaching.

A waiter opened the door and waited with obsequious patience. The legs lengthened, to be topped by a body and then a head. Jenner had the kind of face that made one wonder if perhaps Neanderthal man had lived on. Immediately behind him was a young woman, half his age. With the sling around his left arm to help provide absolute steadiness, Doe studied Jenner's crudely formed face. Seen in profile, his strangely shaped nose was the most notable feature. Had he been called Turnip at school? Nicknames could be bitterly cruel. Doe's had been Washy, derived from wishy-washy. The name still had the power to make him mentally cringe; that was, except when about to prove how inappropriate it was.

Jenner shook hands with the newly visible maître d'. Reputation said he chased the dollars so hard, he'd sell his mother into slavery if he could find anyone who wanted an eighty-year-old harpy for a slave. He moved forward into the doorway, nodded at the waiter who held the door, paused to say something more to the maître d', stepped out onto the pavement. The woman was now behind him.

Doe slid the safety catch forward and hooked his forefinger around the trigger, lined up the cross-wires on Jenner's forehead. Expectant pleasure was like a draught of nectar and he waited, prolonging the pleasure, until an approaching car slowed to a stop and Jenner half turned towards it. As the driver stepped out, preparatory to opening the rear door, Doe squeezed the trigger more gently than any nipple. The explosion in the confine of the room was an aural hammer blow and McCleary expressed his shock with violent swearing; Doe hardly heard him as, fascinated, he watched the miracle of death. The back of Jenner's head had burst open and the woman behind him was splattered with some of the contents; for a split second the body stayed upright, then it collapsed.

"Let's go," McCleary said hoarsely.

Doe moved the rifle to bring the woman's face into the sights. Shock had turned it ugly. She raised a finger to her cheek and touched a lump of something, but seemed to find it impossible to flick away whatever it was. She screamed.

"For Christ's sake, move!"

He lowered the rifle, disengaged his left arm from the sling. McCleary was panicking, which highlighted his stupidity. When the visually and emotionally horrifying happened, all those who witnessed it went into shock. It would take a little time before the police were called; it would take the police much more time to work out what had happened and where the shot had come from. He opened the gun and caught the ejected cartridge, then drew the second, live round out of the left-hand barrel; he put both cases in his trouser pocket. He broke the gun and packed the three parts into the case.

They went downstairs and out into the car park, along the passage to the road and the waiting Jaguar.

"What took you so bloody long?" Rayner asked wildly. "Every copper in the county will be on the way in by now."

"He's slower than a sodding tortoise," McCleary said resentfully.

Doe laughed. "Why the panic? It'll be another quarter of an hour before things calm down enough for the law to begin to work out what happened."

Rayner drove quietly despite the urge to get the hell out of town. They were at the top end of the High Street when a police car, blue lights flashing, passed at speed in the opposite direction.

Rayner brought the Jaguar to a halt in front of the short, mock York stone path that led up to cabin 17, a shingle-clad building identical to the others which lined the circular road.

"Got the Viagras?" Rayner asked; rough humour had replaced nervousness.

"Coals to Newcastle." Doe, gun case in left hand, climbed onto the pavement.

McCleary lowered his window. "Have a bang for me, mate."

"I'll have two for each of you and the rest for myself."

The car drove off and Doe began to walk up the path. The spirit of rough camaraderie would be gone by the morning. It never lasted. Their contempt would return, in part to bolster their self-esteem.

As he neared the front door, tension made him feel weak. He would have had difficulty in hitting a stationary elephant at a hundred yards.

Six

Ballard was passing the senior officers' canteen – the tradition amongst lower ranks was that the fare served there was never less than lobster and T-bone steaks – when Detective Inspector Lock stepped out into the passage.

"Just the man," he said, in his clipped voice which carried just a hint of the local accent.

Ballard came to a halt.

"I need a witness statement from a Mrs Golding, thirty-six Evesham Street, Sergholt; she witnessed a break-in next door. We need as good a description as possible of the two men involved. Apparently she's no chicken, so take things quietly."

"Right, sir. What was the name of the road again?"

"Evesham Street." The DI's tone made it clear Ballard should not have needed to ask. He hurried along the passage and turned right, to go out of sight.

One black mark, Ballard thought, as he followed at a slow enough pace to ensure they would not share the lift; an efficient detective never needed to be told anything twice. The DI, reputedly when appointed the youngest ever to hold that rank in the county force, demanded efficiency in everything at all times. The ranks cursed him for a hard taskmaster, but if pressed accepted that he worked himself as hard as he did others. He had a reputation. As a PC, he had blown the whistle on three fellow PCs who'd bundled a villain into a van and beaten him up because he'd stuck a knife into their mate, then reported that he'd suffered the bruising while resisting arrest. To shop one's own was to breach the code of *omerta*. In the past, his action would have resulted in ostracisation and resignation from the force would have been his only relief. But, however slowly, the ethos was changing and although there were still those who would never forget or forgive, most accepted that he had had to speak up – justice could only be served by the just.

It was generally believed he would reach high rank; perhaps even that pinnacle of police service, appointment as Commissioner for the Metropolitan Police. It was agreed that that was to be welcomed since it would ensure the removal of his hard, sharp, unforgiving presence from the county.

The lift was gone by the time Ballard reached the door and he had a two-minute wait before it returned. Frost was in his office, struggling with the eternal paperwork.

"Morning, Sarge."

"What's good about it?"

"All's made glorious summer by this sun of Kent."

"What the hell are you on about?"

"That's a weak paraphrase of a line from *Richard the Third*."

"Son of Kent, *Richard the Third*. Have you gone round the bloody twist?"

"Just rejoicing because it's a lovely day."

"Then you can rejoice a bit more and take all these two-four-three forms and fill 'em in. And make a mistake, you do the whole thing again." Frost reached across the desk to pick up a bundle of papers.

"I would if I could, Sarge, but I can't. The Guv'nor's just told me to go out and get a witness statement."

"Then why come in here and babble?"

"You said I wasn't to take a CID car without your say-so because last time . . ."

"You drove off for something unimportant and five minutes later Tom was left standing with a heavy job waiting . . . Walk or take a bus."

"Mrs Golding lives in Sergholt. I don't know what sort of bus service there is, but to walk it will take hours."

Frost muttered something, resumed the work he'd been doing.

Assuming permission had been given, Ballard left and made his way downstairs. At times, perhaps at most times, Frost was a discontented man. Because of his nature, or perhaps the result of a tension he didn't fully recognise? He firmly believed the old ways of policing were the best and seemed unable to accept that he must now work under many constraints. One thing was for certain – he wouldn't regret retirement.

One of the Fords was in the car park and Ballard settled behind the wheel. The sun was shining, roses in bloom, flowers a carpet of colour. 'Bliss was it in that dawn to be alive, But to be young was very heaven!' He laughed. Of all the people to misquote poetry to, Frost was the last. He probably equated poetry with queers . . . He stared through the windscreen at the poorly maintained strip of grass which separated the parking area from the surrounding railings. Pleasure unsuspected was twice the pleasure. When he'd last arrived at Ash Farm, Fleur had clearly been excited, but when he'd asked what was up, she'd smiled and said he had to wait.

Her parents had been at home. He could be certain that still in the backs of their minds was the question: since he'd come down from university with a good degree, what had prompted him to join the police? The force was not really socially acceptable. He'd tried, and failed, to explain the satisfaction he gained from knowing, however small his part, he was helping to maintain law and order which was the only way of keeping civilisation civilised, and that for him and his contemporaries social acceptance was unimportant. Perhaps they could half understand the first, but not the second . . .

When he'd entered the sitting room, they'd both greeted him warmly, then Fleur's father had asked him what he'd like to drink. Being thirsty, he'd asked for a lager. They'd only started to have lager in the house after he'd met Fleur – for them, lager spoke of package holidays in Torremolinos. No one had drunk until her father had proposed his usual toast, *A votre santé* (he was a great admirer of French tradition, though not of the French), which provided a sharp contrast to the etiquette in the police club, where one drank as soon as one had a glass. Then her father had continued: "We've something to say to you, Geoffrey."

He'd known a second's foreboding, but had noticed that Fleur's eyes were dancing – a pedant would claim eyes couldn't dance, but hers could.

"As you perhaps know, I've been lucky enough to have some shares which have greatly increased in value."

"So Fleur said when she asked if I'd like some port the other evening."

"It's a pity you didn't. Still, I'm grateful you said no, on two counts. One, there's more for me; two, the thought of its not being fully appreciated would be a painful one." Pearce had smiled.

Ballard had smiled back as he wondered if the other had always been pompous or had that come with age?

"Because of this good luck, Winifred and I have decided to give you our wedding present now, rather than leave it to the day, because it will be more useful to you. We'll be transferring ten thousand pounds to Fleur's bank account to put towards buying a house. This may take a little time to organise because there's the problem of capital transfer tax, but I'm hopeful my financial adviser will be able to suggest a way of avoiding that." He'd paused. "As a reasonable man, I realise taxation is necessary, but when its objective is to prevent one financially helping one's own, I see no cause for recrimination in doing everything legally possible to avoid it."

And so said every sane person. He'd found it difficult to express the measure of his surprised gratitude, but must have succeeded because Fleur's eyes had continued to dance for the rest of the evening, Pearce had been jovial, and Winifred had discussed who should be invited to the wedding. When he'd said goodnight, outside the house and in the cover of a moonless night, she'd whispered: "Not so long to wait as you thought." Her kisses told him she was not referring to their buying a house . . .

"I suppose you think you get paid for sitting on your arse?"

The crude words jerked him free of memories and he turned his head to face the detective sergeant through the opened window. "I was just thinking . . ."

"That's the problem with blokes on special entry – they think they're paid to think."

"I was trying to work out . . ."

"Work yourself out of here bloody quick sharp."

He started the engine, and reversed until he could swing the car round and head for the exit. Frost's sourness didn't begin to spoil the day. He hummed the tune to which Fleur and he had first danced together.

As Doe had judged, when Rayner, driving Cairns's Mercedes (the stolen Jaguar was already well on its way to Poland), had picked him up from the motel all suggestion of camaraderie had vanished, despite the fact that he was careful to sit in the front passenger seat. Much of the drive south was made in silence, but when he spoke, Rayner made clear his resentment at having to act as chauffeur.

When they reached Benwood, they came to a halt in the car park of a large pub on the outskirts.

"What's up?" Doe asked.

"I need a drink."

"But we can't have far to go . . ."

"If I want a drink, I sodding well will have one."

"The sooner I get away, the better for everyone."

"So why spend the night shacked up with a tart?"

There could be no response to that.

Rayner climbed out, slammed the door shut and crossed to the square, shapeless public house.

Time passed. Doe, now nervous, constantly looked at his watch and mentally tried to work out when they'd arrive – a fruitless exercise since he didn't know exactly how far they still had to go.

Rayner finally returned. He started the engine and engaged Drive, released the handbrake.

"How long will it take to get to Gransere?" Doe asked.

Rayner drove round in a circle to reach the exit, waited for a van to pass, drew out onto the road.

"How long will it take?" Doe asked a second time.

"What's it matter?" Rayner belched.

Doe settled back in his seat. In truth, it probably didn't matter if they arrived after the arranged time. He let his mind wander. In his second case was a small fortune in used dollar notes – his payment. Money had magical powers; it could turn a frog into a prince. In Viniscola, less than twenty kilometres from Port de Majerda, there were people who treated him with great respect . . .

They turned off the A-road into a lane.

His feeling of contentment ceased. "What's up?"

"I'm taking a short cut," Rayner answered shortly.

"How d'you know it is?"

"What's that to do with you? Who's driving? Lived here when I was young, didn't I?"

They passed through a village set about crossroads that consisted of four houses, three bungalows, and a pub.

"I've had a few pints there," Rayner said suddenly, as they came abreast of the pub.

"It looks old."

He made no effort to continue the conversation.

The road was almost straight for a mile, then in a wide turn it climbed a short, shallow hill. Sited along the crest of this was another village, considerably larger than the previous one, with a general store, garage, butchers, pub, school and playing field.

"Played cricket there," Rayner said, with a jerk of the head to the left.

Doe looked at the pitch and the crude pavilion and found great difficulty in envisaging Rayner's doing anything so peaceful.

The road made a sweeping left-hand turn between high banks, on top of which grew several ancient oaks, and then rose into a right-hand bend. Rayner left the bend well into his side of the road and at little more than twenty-five miles an hour.

There was a house to their left and fifty feet beyond a tithe barn; access to the farmyard was through a wide gateway, and as they passed the house a boy on a motor scooter, clearly having lost control, shot out of the gateway and onto the road in front of the Mercedes.

Reacting very quickly, Rayner desperately tried to avoid a collision and swung the wheel over to the right. But despite all his skill, the crash was unavoidable. There was a thump, a screech of metal, the back of the car rose and fell as the rear wheel rode over something. A dry skid threatened to slam them into a grass verge, high enough to be dangerous. Using reverse lock and pumping the brakes, he succeeded in avoiding the verge by inches. As he straightened up the car, he said, his voice strained: "What about the kid?"

Doe undid the seat belt and twisted round to stare through the rear-view window. "It's impossible to be certain. He's just lying there."

"I couldn't do anything. There wasn't no chance of missing him. Is there anyone else around?"

Doe checked. "An old man in the garden of the cottage."

"He could've seen." Rayner began to brake.

"Are you suicidal? Keep going."

"But it wasn't my fault . . ."

"D'you want to explain to the fuzz who we are and where we're heading?"

Rayner moved his foot off the brake pedal and accelerated. They rounded a bend to pass out of sight of the crash.

It took the unexpected to expose the true man, Doe thought. Rayner, who liked to think he was so tough he could crack walnuts between his toes, had threatened to put the operation in jeopardy merely because he'd run over a kid.

Seven

Carlo Giulio's born name was Daniel Easton, but if one was running an Italian restaurant it seemed sensible to have an Italian name. "But I must know," he said plaintively.

"You'll hear in time to boil up the macaroni," replied the detective sergeant.

"But my customers . . ."

"Won't die of starvation."

"I have bookings . . ."

"Take him away and explain in simple language," said the detective inspector wearily.

The detective sergeant led Easton across to the far side of the restaurant where they sat at a table which, on police orders, had not been cleared. The detective sergeant picked up a roll, broke off the end with his fingers and used a knife to butter this. He ate. "You serve stale rolls?"

They were all crazy, Easton thought despairingly; determined to feast at his funeral. With Jenner dead, there was no knowing what would happen to the restaurant and his job.

The detective superintendent, followed by the detective inspector, went out on to the pavement, part of which had been sectioned off by plastic police tape. He looked down at the bloody stain and the chalk marks outlining a body, then across the road and up at the window on the third floor from which it had been established the shot had been fired. "You say this restaurant is owned by Jenner?"

"I've a bloke confirming that, sir, but it's taking time because Jenner's operations are complex. A smart operator."

"But not quite smart enough. Is there anything in from Ballistics yet?"

"They promise a report very soon. Off the record, the rifle was high velocity, probably a sporting model because of the unusual calibre, firing a bullet fashioned to cause maximum destruction and far more effective than the old-fashioned dumdum. Obviously, a bullet that's not commercially available."

"Made by whoever fired the shot?"

"More like a specialist supplier."

The detective superintendent lowered his gaze. "Ghouls," he said.

It took the detective inspector a moment to realise the comment was directed at the onlookers who stood on the pavement. How they'd scatter in panic if another shot were fired!

"The man who fired obviously didn't think a second shot was necessary as insurance."

"Using the ammo he was, that's not surprising."

"An expert, brought in on what must have been a pricey contract, because Jenner had become too ambitious and was trying to enlarge his territory? Is that how you see it at the moment?"

"Yes, sir. And I'd say there's confirmation in the talk that a shipment of E meant for Cairns was recently hijacked by his mob."

"Just talk?"

"We've been digging hard, but not turned up anything specific as yet."

"What are you proposing to do about Cairns?"

"Everything we can. We'll be questioning him and his lads and tapping all the snouts to find out if any of his lot have been seen in the company of a known hit man."

"Is he still run from abroad?"

"As far as we can judge, Hastings, who's said to live in Spain, still controls strategically."

"Getting ever richer as he enjoys the sun, sea, and sangria?"

"Not to forget the sex."

"An unnecessary comment," snapped the detective superintendent.

The DI had heard him crack jokes as crude as they came. But one of the benefits of rank was the right to be inconsistent.

The ambulance left. The driver of the patrol car watched the boy's father put his arm around the mother and slowly lead her back into the house. She had wanted to go in the ambulance with her son, but had been persuaded not to by the crew, but to follow by car. That meant the boy was either dying or dead.

He walked across to where an elderly man, with a face pitted by years and an outdoor life, waited. "Right, Mr Aldridge, sorry to keep you waiting. What say we sit in the car?"

They settled in the front of the patrol car parked in the farm entrance. The Police Code of Discipline made it clear that smoking was not permitted on duty, but it was unlikely that any senior officer would appear; the PC produced a pack of cigarettes. "D'you want one?"

Aldridge hesitated, then took one. The PC flicked open a lighter and they both lit up. Aldridge began to cough. "The doctor says I shouldn't smoke," he wheezed.

"They're always trying to make life miserable." The PC was not yet old enough to worry about the effects of lifestyle.

"Me dad smoked all his life and his brothers was the same and it was old age did 'em in, not smoking. Like me mother's family . . ."

The PC listened for a while to an involved genealogical and medical history, then his patience failed. "Suppose we talk about what happened?" He picked up his notebook from the top of the dashboard, uncapped a ball-point pen.

Aldridge, baffled by the array of dials, switches, radio controls, and VDU screen, looked around for an ashtray. Poor old bastard, lost in the modern world, the PC thought. "Chuck the ash out of the window, but make certain none blows back inside." He activated the electric switch and the nearside window slid down. "Now, as I understand things, you live in the cottage just down the road – is that right?"

"Been there fifty-one year. Moved in when I was married . . ."

"And you were in the garden when you saw the car come round the corner?" he cut in quickly, before being given a history of the marriage.

"That's right."

"What were you doing?"

"Gardening. The old woman likes the flower beds to be clear. Many's the time I've said to her, where's the point when you can't eat—"

"Was the car going very quickly?"

"Not nearly as fast as some of 'em what don't worry about other people. There was a time when—"

"So why did you look at it?"

The question puzzled Aldridge. A countryman, he was interested in anything and everything that went on.

"Tell me what happened after you first saw the car."

"I see Simon . . ." He stopped. His lower jaw, prickled with grey stubble, moved as if he were chewing something; his watery eyes became unfocused.

"You saw Simon?"

"He came out on that new motor scooter his dad give him. Came out of the yard and straight in front of the car."

"How far from the car would you reckon he was when he first reached the road?"

For some reason, he was unwilling to give even a rough

42

estimate; all he'd say was that the driver of the car couldn't
have avoided Simon. The car had swerved, but it wasn't any
use; it had hit the scooter and then run over Simon. It were
really terrible . . .

"Very nasty," the PC said. "What did the car do?"

The car had slowed, then speeded up and gone round the
next corner.

"Wasn't nothing I could do but read the number."

"You what?" said the PC surprised.

"Read the number. Wasn't that right?"

"I'd say it's the smartest thing you've done in a month of
Sundays. So what was it?"

"The number?"

"That's right."

"I've forgotten. I can't remember things these days."

There were times, the PC thought, when involuntary eutha-
nasia was probably justified. "So you can't now give me any
of the numbers or letters?"

"I can tell you 'em all."

"I'm just not on your wavelength. First you say you read
the number, then you can't remember it, then you can tell me
it. I mean, make your mind up."

"Like I said, I ain't so good with memory these days, so
I called out to the old woman and told her to write the
number down."

"Very sensible. So she'll be able to tell me what it was?"

"That's right."

"And where is she now?"

"In the house, like as not."

"I'll have a word with her later on. Let's now talk about the
car. Can you say what make it was?"

"It were large. That's all I know." He explained at length that
when he'd been young different makes of cars were different,
now they all looked the same. He had a collection of cigarette

cards from before the war, in an album, which showed the various makes and they were as different as could be . . .

"What was the colour?" the PC hurriedly asked.

"Green."

"That's about it, then." He closed the notebook, capped the pen. "Thanks for your time. And I'll be along in a while to find out what your wife wrote down."

Aldridge left the car, then leaned over and said through the opened window: "Can you say how Simon is?"

"Afraid not. Not been time for the doctors to find out and let us know."

"I hopes he lives. A bright lad."

"It's usually the bright ones," the PC said meaninglessly. "Suppose you go along to your place and tell your missus I'll be around soon?" He was relieved when Aldridge walked away with stumping stride; a long discussion about the victim had been avoided.

Frost stood in front of the detective inspector's desk; only occasionally was anyone asked to sit. "From the eyewitness's report, there can't be much doubt that Simon Kerr came out of the gateway and straight in front of the oncoming car, leaving the driver no realistic chance of avoiding him."

"Then why didn't the car stop?"

"Maybe the driver panicked, he'd told his wife he was hard at work fifty miles away, he just reckoned it wasn't his fault so he'd not stay around to get caught up in all the hassle."

"He must have known it was his duty to stop at the scene of an accident in which he was involved, whether or not he was to blame."

The DI, Frost thought wearily, seemed to imagine that the ordinary honest citizen lived by the rule book. Experience should have convinced him that the ordinary honest citizen always took the easy way out provided he could find justification for doing so.

"There was only the one eyewitness?"

"The Kerr parents were inside and there's not another house along that stretch of road."

"So we have to rely on—" The DI looked down at the report Frost had earlier given him – "Aldridge. He's pretty ancient."

"They do say wine matures in the bottle."

"What?"

"Just a thought, sir."

"Leave the literary pretensions to Ballard."

"I had a word with PC Ingham. Aldridge is on the wrong side of seventy, but mentally must still be around since he had the initiative to take the car's number."

"He admits to a poor memory."

"Which is why he told his wife to write down the number he gave her. A combined effort, you could call it."

"Have you asked for an identification of the owner?"

"Yes, sir."

Lock looked down at the paper, then up. "Let me know the moment you hear from Swansea."

Frost returned to his office next door and, since his legs quickly became tired these days, was glad to sit. Lock never relaxed, never lost the edge of his sharpness. He'd be a real bastard in high office. But to give him his due, an efficient real bastard.

On the desk was a doctor's certificate to the effect that DC York had suffered a sprained ankle and would be off work for an as yet indeterminate time. What with sprained ankles, holidays, attendances at special courses, and trial appearances, soon there would be no active CID left . . .

The phone rang. The registration number belonged to a four-month-old white Astra, owned by Gerald Underwood who lived at 6 Knightsbridge Road, Carske, Yorkshire.

He thanked the caller, replaced the receiver. An Astra was generally considered to be a medium sized, not a large car, but estimated size was a matter of individual judgement; far more pertinent was the fact that Aldridge had named the car green. It looked as if his memory had slipped in between reading the letters and figures and shouting them to his wife. However, one had to be certain. And since the inquiries would be made by the West Yorkshire police, he was quite content that this was so.

Ballard brought his ancient Escort to a stop. "There we are."

Fleur stared through the windscreen at the site on which a dozen houses were being built around a horseshoe-shaped road. "What a mess!"

"Things usually are at this stage."

"The houses are going to be very close together. How much are they going to cost?"

"Eighty to ninety thousand depending on which of the interiors one chooses."

"It seems an awful lot of money for . . ."

"Something you'd hate?"

She reached across and took hold of his left hand. "Not hate."

"But it's not a country cottage with beamed ceilings and the scent of history."

"You think I'm being stupid?"

"In two words, im-possible."

"Try sounding a little more convincing . . . I am being stupid because there's just no way we can afford to buy somewhere like Ash Farm, yet every time we look at somewhere in town I think of green fields."

"And beamed ceilings?"

She leaned across and kissed him on the cheek. "Stop mocking me." She squeezed his hand, then sat back and stared

46

through the windscreen once more. "I suppose it'll all look better when it's finished."

"But no less suburban. If I were an accountant, as your father was, I could buy the kind of house you want," he said, his tone briefly resentful.

"But you're not one because you're doing what you want and that's far more important than the kind of house we live in."

"Is it?"

"Yes, yes, yes."

"I don't think you really believe that."

"Are you forgetting we promised always to believe each other because we'd always tell the truth?"

"Perhaps you are misjudging your own emotions."

"That's better." She laughed.

When she laughed, he stepped aboard cloud nine . . .

"What are you thinking?"

"That I love you so much I could dance on water."

"Let's drive down to the lake now so I can watch you."

"There has to be an R in the month . . . I've decided what to do. I'll win the Lottery tomorrow and buy Thornton Abbey and you'll have history and green fields in profusion."

"Is it for sale?"

"According to the local paper. Two and a quarter million and the best estimate is that another million will be needed on restoration."

"I wouldn't want to live in somewhere that enormous."

"Excuse my saying so, but you're very difficult to please!"

"But just think of trying to keep all those rooms clean and tidy. There'd be no time for anything else."

"In that case, I certainly won't buy you the Abbey."

There was a brief silence, which she broke. "Darling . . ."

"Yes?"

"You do really understand, don't you? Wherever we live is

going to be home and I'll be happy. It's just that . . . Mother says I'm a romantic dreamer."

"Who doesn't want to live in this close. You're probably right. It already has a sanctimonious air."

"We'll find somewhere we both really like."

"With a little luck."

"Of course we will. Maybe I do dream, but I can be very practical. Saying which, we'd better return to the flat so I can cook supper."

"What's on the menu? A dozen oysters, *bœuf en croûte*, and *glacé noisette*?"

"Now who's the romantic dreamer?"

Eight

The call from the West Yorkshire police came through at midday on Saturday.

"We've questioned Mr Underwood and, with his permission, inspected his car. He and his wife drove over to friends and were there from eleven to after four in the afternoon. The friends confirm this. The car shows no sign of damage."

"So that puts them in the clear and us without a case. Thanks for your help," Frost said.

"I'd answer 'any time', but it would be a lie."

He said goodbye, replaced the receiver. No one was going to be surprised that Aldridge's evidence proved to be unreliable. In practical terms, the case was now dead, but because the DI was so sharp it would not be buried until further inquiries made certain nothing which might identify the car had been missed – the DI would have demanded confirmatory evidence that it was Anne Boleyn's head which had been chopped off her body.

When Ballard had been told he was to be transferred from uniform to temporary plain-clothes service where he would deal with minor matters, so leaving the regular members of CID to work on major cases, he had experienced a frisson of excitement; even for men with many years' service, plain-clothes duty held a cachet – ironically, in part because of television series in which detectives battled with the forces of evil and never lost. It had needed very little time to discover the down side to the work. Hours were long and irregular; there could be considerable tension and the easiest way of releasing this was with drink, so that many became alcoholics; family life could be severely disrupted, with the result that the rate of break-up of marriages was well above the national average . . .

"It's Saturday and my afternoon off, Sarge," he protested.

"It was," Frost replied.

"Fleur and I are going for a drive . . ."

"It doesn't matter if the Queen's invited you for a trip in the state carriage, we're short-handed because clumsy oafs trip up and twist their ankles."

"We've fixed to see friends of her parents who've said they may be selling a cottage which they've been letting and is soon to become vacant. It's small and not particularly old, but it's in the country and there aren't any other houses really close. We're hoping that as they're family friends, they won't quote a ridiculous price."

"Ever the wide-eyed optimist!"

Ballard persevered. "If we don't turn up, they'll think we're not interested and that'll be that."

"You're breaking my heart."

"Sarge, be human. It's not as if the case is a major one, even if the poor kid did die. All the driver of the car seems to be guilty of is not stopping after the accident. So even if we do manage to identify him . . ."

"Which we won't all the time you keep standing there."

"What I'm saying is, in something this minor, surely there can be a little leeway of time?"

"Would you like to ask the DI if he agrees with that?"

He was silent.

Frost sighed. "I wish I knew why I'm such a sucker for a bleeding-heart story. All right, get out to Clevestone tomorrow morning . . ."

"That'll be Sunday and—"

"Haven't you ever heard about the horrible history of the bear cub which wouldn't learn to stop asking for honey? Tomorrow morning, question Aldridge and see if there's any chance of judging whether he misread just one number or letter, or if it was the whole bloody lot. And then have a word with the parents. Did they try to teach the boy some road sense? The motor scooter was new, but had they checked the brakes were working? The Coroner will want to know the answers."

"Do we have to question them so soon after the accident?"

"Yes."

A job, Ballard thought bitterly, that was bound to prove distressing and given to him, although he had no experience of such a duty, because he was the junior in CID.

He drove out of the car park in the CID Rover and went down past the railway station and through south Staple Cross. Beyond the town were thorn hedges, single trees, copses, woods, and villages. Small wonder that Fleur wanted to continue to live in the countryside. Would she have the chance? The family friends had been strangely reluctant to discuss a possible price if they did put the cottage up for sale. On their drive back, Fleur had suggested that this was because they were of the generation that had been brought up never to mix business with social pleasure. He'd wondered if the more likely explanation was that they were hoping to sell it for more than Fleur and he could obviously afford. He cursed his inability to buy her a dream house; tried and failed to console himself with the thought that instead of complaining, he should be grateful for the benefits they were lucky enough to enjoy.

He passed through Clevestone, and when the Kerrs' farm-house came into sight his immediate thought was that here was somewhere which would fulfil Fleur's every romantic dream. The steeply pitched peg-tile roof, high, spindly, shaped chimney stack, exposed timbers, and variegated bricks, had outlived many, many centuries – the house was history . . . Yet for the Kerrs it would have become a place of bitter sorrow. The cottage beyond was no more than a couple of centuries old and very much smaller, but it possessed the same quality of seeming to belong to the land. He parked the car, opened the rusting metal gate, and walked up the path to the front door. His knock was answered by an old woman whose white hair was sparse and her face a confused mass of lines. "Mrs Aldridge? Morning, my name's Detective Constable Ballard, local CID." Officially, he was still PC Ballard, but he allowed himself the inaccuracy.

"You want a word with Bert?"

"If that's all right?"

"He's watching the telly."

He stepped into a very small hall, on two walls of which hung framed hunting prints. She opened the door on her right. "Bert, it's the police," she said as she went into the room.

Ballard followed her and the first thing he noticed was that Aldridge was wearing glasses.

"Turn the telly off," she said.

"But it's me favourite programme."

"Never mind that."

Mumbling to himself, he used the remote control to switch off the set.

"Sit down, then," she said. "And would you like some tea?"

"No thanks." Ballard settled on an armchair that had a spring loose in the seat.

"I'll leave you 'cause I've cooking to do." She quickly moved forward and picked up a newspaper that was on the arm of the settee, put this on the central glass-topped table, left.

"I'm sorry to spoil your television," Ballard said.

"I always watch me favourite programme," Aldridge replied sulkily.

"Maybe there'll be a repeat."

"Don't expect so."

It was not a good beginning. "I won't keep you for long and then I'll be away and leave you in peace."

"Me programme will be finished by then."

"Hopefully not. I'm here because of the distressing accident – must have been a nasty shock for you."

"Aye."

"I need to ask some more questions because we're trying to trace the driver of the car that knocked Simon over and should have stopped after the accident."

Aldridge continued to stare at the blank television screen.

"I know you've helped us already, but what you've told us raises a problem. You were smart enough to read the registration number and get your wife to note that down, but we've checked and found that the car with that number was up North at the time of the accident, so you must have made a mistake."

"Like I said, I did me best."

"Of course you did. No question . . . Tell me, were you wearing glasses when the accident happened?"

"Don't really need 'em except for the telly. But like he said . . ." He became silent.

"What did he say?"

"If I wasn't wearing me glasses, things couldn't be as sharp as they might be, but it wasn't everyone what would have tried to read the number. And if maybe I couldn't be real certain what I'd seen, no one could blame me."

It was clear that Aldridge had accepted he could have been mistaken even before it was obvious he had. "Have you any idea what number or letter you might most easily have mistaken?"

"Don't know what you're at."

Ballard explained that experience might have taught him what he was most likely to muddle when not wearing distance glasses.

"Like he said to me, M and N can look alike. And nought and eight. And there was something more only I can't remember."

He was very surprised that Warren Ingham could have conducted so ham-fisted an interview that it was almost as if he'd done his best to persuade Aldridge that because he had not been wearing glasses he could not have read the number correctly. Ingham was always full of himself, so it was going to be amusing to pull his leg and advise him against joining CID. "The police constable said all this to you immediately after the accident?"

"It were after dark."

"But the accident was soon after midday."

"I know that."

"Then it wasn't dark, was it?"

"I know that as well, not being daft."

"Then I don't follow what you're saying."

"He came after dark, didn't he? And interrupted me favourite programme on the telly."

It seemed he had many favourite programmes. "You're saying the PC questioned you a second time?"

"No, I ain't. Never seen him before."

A touch of surrealism seemed to have crept into the conversation. Ballard wondered if he'd been misled into according Aldridge more intelligence than was his due. "Are you saying a policeman questioned you late Friday night, but he wasn't the police constable who spoke to you immediately after the accident at midday?"

"Ain't that what I've just told?"

In the progress report of the case, there had been no mention of this second questioning which had led to Aldridge's having doubts about the accuracy of his reading of the car's registration number. Yet this bore heavily on the question of how much weight to give to his evidence. "Who let him into the house?"

"Me. The old woman was out at some meeting at the village hall. Goes off and leaves me on my own, she does. All the time. It ain't right at my age . . ."

"Was he in uniform?"

"No."

CID. Yet clearly Frost did not know that a member of CID had questioned Aldridge for a second time, on the night of the accident. "What was his name?"

"Don't remember. Me memory ain't what it used to be."

"Did he show you his warrant card?"

"Could of done."

"You can't be certain?"

Aldridge's expression became sullen.

"He pointed out that if you weren't wearing glasses, you might not have been able to read all the letters and numbers correctly?"

"I said, I don't need me glasses for gardening."

"Will you describe this man to me?"

"I ain't good at describing."

"It is very difficult to give a word picture of someone, but perhaps you can recall some of his features?"

"My memory ain't what it used to be."

"So you said before."

"I don't never remember faces."

"But I'm sure you can say how old you reckon he was?"

"Weren't as old as me."

"My age, perhaps?"

"Older than you. A good bit older."

"Was he a tall or a short man?"

"Likely he was a fair bit taller than me."

"Six feet or more?"

"Maybe."

"Thin, fat?"

"Could've been like you."

He considered himself to be well built. "Were his ears pointed or rounded?"

"How would I know that?"

"Then you didn't notice if they lay close to his head or stuck out?"

"No."

"What colour was his hair?"

"Couldn't say."

"Black, brown, red?"

"I said . . ."

"I know you did, Mr Aldridge, but sometimes with a little prompting, a witness can remember something he didn't realise he still knew."

There was a long pause as Aldridge continued to stare at the television set, his expression almost as blank as the screen. "I reckon it was black," he finally said. "And maybe a bit wavy like."

"What shape of face – oval, round, square?"

"Just ordinary."

"Was he clean shaven?"

"How would I know?"

Ballard spoke with commendable patience. "Did he have a moustache or a beard?"

"Oh! . . . No."

"Did he have a big nose?"

"Can't remember . . . No, that's a lie. It did stick out a bit."

"Was it straight or crooked?"

He shrugged his shoulders.

"Was his mouth large, did he have thick lips?"

"I keep telling you, I don't remember because my memory ain't as good as it was. When I was a youngster . . ."

"Did he speak with a local accent?"

Aldridge sighed. "I can't say, can I?"

Ballard continued to question him, but learned nothing. At the end, he said: "If you saw him again, would you recognise him?"

"Might do," he answered, with such little certainty it seemed clear he probably would not.

"That's it, then." Ballard stood. "I can leave you to your favourite programme."

"It'll be over," he muttered as he reached for the remote control.

Ballard thanked him, said goodbye, left.

As he settled behind the wheel of the Rover, he tried to identify who had questioned Aldridge on the Friday night. None of the DCs in R Division were much older than he, roughly his height and build, and had black, wavy hair. In the uniform branch, there was a PC with so many years' service his nickname was Methuselah, but since he still spoke with a Geordie accent, even Aldridge, with his colander memory, must surely have remembered that. Could the questioner, however unlikely, have been from another division? But as a matter of courtesy, such a foray would have been advised in advance.

He started the engine, checked the road was clear and made a three-point turn. As he approached Enton Farm, his reluctance at questioning the Kerrs increased.

Nine

Ballard entered the detective sergeant's room. "I had a word with Mr Aldridge yesterday morning."

Frost put down the memorandum he had been reading. "They're round the bloody twist. Or have shares in paper-making companies. There's new advice concerning statements made before any charge has been laid. An extra form to be filled out in triplicate . . . What do you want?"

"Like I've just said . . ."

"Then don't say it again."

"Aldridge accepts he probably read the registration number incorrectly."

"Is that supposed to be news? We know he made a cock-up."

"The things is, he wears glasses for the television which probably means he needs 'em for distance, whatever he says. He wasn't wearing 'em Friday midday."

"So who was the dumb bastard who questioned him but didn't find that out?"

"I'm not sure." One tried never to land a fellow ranker in the mud. "But it's understandable. When you see a bloke without glasses and there's no reason to think he can't see clearly, you don't ask him if he ever needs 'em."

"Depends if your IQ reaches up to double figures."

"Straight, you get called to an incident and everyone's so stressed you can't think of everything."

"And there's some who can't think of anything . . . I suppose Aldridge now reckons he got things wrong because ten minutes with you would confuse anyone?"

"It wasn't me who confused him, it was whoever called at his place Friday night."

"Who did?"

"I don't know."

"And of course it never occurred to you to ask?"

"Someone called at the house and said he was a policeman, but if he gave his name, Aldridge has forgotten it. He was watching television and so was wearing glasses, this policeman spent time pointing out that since he hadn't been wearing 'em when he read the car's number, he was likely to have mixed up letters like M and N and figures like nought and eight."

"In uniform?"

"Civvies."

Frost tapped on the desk with his fingers. "I didn't detail anyone to go along since there wasn't any point before we heard from Swansea. There's been no cross-divisional visit. So who the hell was he?"

"I tried to get a description, but as Aldridge said many times, his memory's not what it was. The best he could come up with was much older then me, about my build, black hair that's maybe wavy, and a bit of a noticeable nose."

"That doesn't fit anyone in this manor. Have we got a bogus copper going around?"

"I wondered that, but why go to the Aldridges? I doubt there's anything in the house that wouldn't collect the scorn of even a hard-up fence. And this bloke seemed to know too many details of the fatal accident for him to be an outsider."

"Are you saying he was a genuine copper?"

"The circumstances seem to suggest he was."

"And he goes along to Aldridge's place and persuades him he couldn't have read the number correctly?"

"Suppose . . ."

"Well?"

"Someone wanted to make certain the person or persons in the car couldn't be identified sufficiently strongly for a case to go to court?"

"Now you're saying he *was* a bent copper?" he said angrily.

"It does seem possible . . ."

"Aldridge couldn't be having fun making you look even stupider than you are?" He spoke more calmly. If pressed, he would reluctantly have admitted that bent coppers were not totally unknown, even in the county force.

"I'm sure it wasn't like that."

Frost slunped back in the chair, his expression now gloomier than usual. "I'll have to pass this on. It's not going to make the guv'nor's day brighter, especially as he all but tore off my necessaries for having detailed you to question Aldridge."

"Why should that cause problems?"

"According to him, I should have been able to judge the case was too weak to waste any more time on it. The bloke who said a detective inspector can do no wrong and a detective sergeant no right knew what he was talking about." He jerked himself upright. "No work to do?"

"More than enough."

"Then go and try to do it."

Ballard crossed to the doorway, came to a stop, turned. "I've just realised something. That description Aldridge gave me does, with imagination, just about fit someone."

"Who?"

"The DI."

"You think that's funny? Suppose you tell him you reckon he's bent and find out just how humorous you are!"

Ballard left. It had been a mistake to imagine Frost would be amused because the idea was so absurd. Whilst he was ready to criticise his superiors, deep down he had an old-fashioned respect for rank.

Ballard was not surprised that Fleur's one regret – he cheerfully assumed it was her only one – over their coming marriage was that she would no longer live at Ash Farm. Rationalists would deny a building an emotional presence, but she believed houses could welcome or spurn and he would not disagree. Ash Farm welcomed. Since the house was over four hundred years old, by the laws of probability it must have experienced tragedies, but clearly these had been outweighed by the happiness its occupants had enjoyed. To be in the sitting room, with its heavily beamed ceiling and wall, was to enjoy a sense of warm continuity.

"Would you like an aperitif, Geoffrey?" Pearce asked.

Very genteel, Ballard thought with an inward smile. In the police canteen it was, "What's your rotgut?" Pearce was a stickler for custom; tall, grey-haired, hawk nosed, a cultured voice, a vaguely distant politeness, and always carefully dressed, he needed only a club tie and a cigar to complete the picture of the archetypal well-bred Englishman who was said to have lived in pre-package-holiday times. Yet he had a generous sense of humour (else why would he have accepted with only mild regret a prospective son-in-law who had been to a red-brick university and not Oxbridge, had read English and not Groats, and joined the police force instead of one of the professions?) . . .

"An apertif, Geoffrey?"

"Wake up," Fleur said.

"Sorry. May I have a gin and tonic, please?"

Pearce turned away to go to the cocktail cabinet that stood in the short passage, on the far side of the massive inglenook fireplace, which ran between the dining and the sitting room.

"Ian," Fleur called out.

It had surprised Ballard when he had first heard her call her father by his Christian name. It marked the independence of her spirit.

"Yes?"

"Have you had a word with the Mountforts?"

"I'll tell you in a minute."

Pearce returned, a silver salver in his right hand. "Where's Winifred?"

"Still in the kitchen," Fleur answered.

"Would you slip through and tell her that drinks are served."

Fleur left, to return almost immediately. "There's a minor crisis and she'd like hers out there."

"I'll take it to her." Pearce handed each of them a glass, left.

Fleur raised her schooner. "Don't let it evaporate."

"Shouldn't we wait for the formal toast?" Ballard asked, only half in jest.

"Naturally. Which is why for once we aren't going to. It's such fun doing something one shouldn't."

"I'll remind you of that at a later hour."

She drank. Her father, ever traditional and often out of date, had guided her to like a dry sherry before a meal.

Pearce returned, put the salver down on the table by the side of his chair, sat. "I see you've started."

"Do you know why?" she asked.

"Of course." Pearce turned to Ballard. "You're going to have to keep a close eye on Fleur's love of rebellion if you're to make certain it doesn't get out of hand."

"Hopefully, time will save me having to do the near impossible."

"'My salad days, When I was green in judgment.'"

Ballard recognised the quotation, but said: "Where's that from?" Pearce enjoyed the chance to air his erudition.

"Shakespeare, but I can't tell you the play. Surprised you didn't know it."

Fleur winked at Ballard. Then she said: "You were going to tell us about the Mountforts. Have they said what they'll do about the cottage?"

"I'm afraid their news wasn't what you'd hoped. The tenant has had second thoughts and says he wants to negotiate a further lease."

"Are they going to agree?"

"As far as I can gather, because it was the first place they lived in after their marriage, Elsa has a sentimental attachment to it so whilst they will sell if it becomes empty, it seems she's happy to have a tenant in it. I couldn't make out what he really thought."

"Shit!"

"You know how I hate hearing you say that sort of thing."

"And I keep trying to make you understand that in this day and age, that's totally mild. What would you rather? That I stamp my foot and say, 'bother', 'blow'?"

"It would be far more elegant."

"And infinitely less satisfying. If you weren't a dinosaur, you'd try some rounded swearing the next time you're screwing two bits of wood together and the head of the screw burrs."

"For your future reference, dinosaurs were so successful that they existed for longer than most other species."

It intrigued Ballard that a family could josh each other to the extent that the Pearces did, yet never provoke ill temper. When his father or mother had appeared to criticise the other, voices had been raised as tempers flared.

"You're wandering again," Fleur said sharply.

"Not really," Ballard protested.

"Yes, you were. Bored by the juvenile level of conversation?"

There were times when he found her sense of humour somewhat embarrassing. "Fascinated by its depth of perception."

Winifred came into the room. "I've finally managed to sort things out. Ian, my glass is empty."

Fleur spoke in mock surprise. "A second drink before the meal?"

Winifred sat. "After the stress of a bad egg in the middle of preparing the sweet, I may even demand a third one."

"I've chosen a good wine for the meal and that calls for an unanaesthetised palate to appreciate it, so your demand will be denied," Pearce said, as he crossed the floor to take her glass.

Ballard wondered how fierce a row that would have provoked in his home.

Ten

B allard was crossing the car park when Frost came out of the building. "Sarge!"

"If there's a panic, tell someone else about it." Frost walked past him.

He turned and followed the other. "Did you have a word with the Guv'nor about the man who called on Aldridge that evening and said he was a policeman?"

"I did and got roundly bollocked for my pains."

"Why?"

"For wasting my time on a case that so very obviously was dead. I tried to explain that I was making certain nothing had been missed, but he wouldn't listen. If I'd done nothing, he'd have bollocked me just the same. Life's a no-win misery."

"Wasn't he concerned at the possibilities?"

"His concern was to decide who's the comedian, you or Aldridge."

They reached the cream-coloured Corsa and Frost opened the driver's door.

"Aldridge wasn't talking nonsense."

"Then according to the DI you were."

"Someone called at the house that evening, claiming to be a policeman."

"If that's what really did happen, it's the oldest ploy in the book for a journalist wanting to edge his way into a story."

"No journalist would try to twist the evidence by persuading Aldridge he couldn't have read the registration number correctly."

"Which he didn't."

"That wasn't known by Friday night."

"You're fixed on saying the man was a bent copper? Is that the kind of loyalty they teach you at university?"

"Loyalty doesn't come into it. If he is a copper, he's got to be exposed for the sake of justice."

"Shouldn't you be standing to attention and saluting whilst you talk like that?"

Ballard felt his face redden.

"You think you're picked out to lead a moral crusade?"

"I can't understand why the DI isn't trying to find out who the man is."

"Because he's not satisfied that Aldridge's evidence can be taken at face value."

"Aldridge isn't a Brain of Britain, but he's not stupid, so why should he make up something like that?"

"He may not be stupid, but he's a ripe old age, which means he gets things muddled. And I don't suppose you've stopped to realise that there's nothing to go on except his description, and if we bring in everyone who fits that, we'll need an army just to control 'em."

"Even so, I'd have expected the DI to—"

"When you learn not to expect, you may start resembling a copper. With nothing to go on, the chances of identifying this bloke are next to nil. The DI has to work to priorities and a good clear-up rate is priority *numero uno*. So unless this bloke surfaces again, or we get a definite lead on him, he remains on the back burner. Think about it."

"I do understand . . ."

"That I should see the day!" Frost climbed into the car,

settled behind the wheel. "Stand clear. I don't want to damage my car by running over you." He slammed the door shut.

Ballard knocked on the window. Reluctantly, Frost lowered it. "What now?"

"Accept Aldridge got everything right; that the man wasn't a journalist looking for a new angle to the story of the accident; that he set out to confuse things to the point where Aldridge's evidence would be so inconsistent and obviously faulty the case would be a no-go. Why would he take the risk when the only offence committed was not stopping after the accident?"

"I don't know," he said wearily, "but I've the feeling that you're going to tell me."

"It must be because identification of the occupants of the car would be dangerous to them and the obvious circumstances in which that would be is if they'd just committed a major crime. I've been checking. Know what I've found?"

"Someone's nicked the Prime Minister's smile."

"The previous evening, Robert Jenner was shot in Childerton by an expert. I reckon it was the hit man in the car."

"You lack a lot of things, but not imagination."

"I've gone on from there. Why would the car have gone through Clevestone, which is off any main road and quite deep in the country? It was going to be obvious the marksman was an expert hit man, and there aren't that many of them around; so if one's found in a car, either on his own or being driven by someone with a record, he's going to be very suspect. So this bloke needed to disappear not only from the law's sight but Jenner's mob, who could be looking for revenge. Using any of the normal exits out of the country would be risky if all ports and airports were alerted, so one solution would be to leave on a yacht; it's summer and thousands of people sail out of ports or marinas every day, which means the chances of being sussed are maybe nil.

"Over the past few years, the marina at Gransere has been

67

developed into one of the biggest on the south coast and that makes it a good departure point. Coming from London, the motorway sweeps well clear of it, so most people leave and continue down on the A-road; but since even that isn't direct, someone who knows what he's doing gets off the A-road early on and cuts through the countryside in a direct route that goes through Clevestone.

"I reckon it's odds on that the man who shot Jenner was in the car, which is why it didn't stop after the accident, and that an identification of the car had to be scrambled to prevent his being fingered."

"How did the people in the car know there was an eye-witness?"

"They saw him."

"How did they find out who he was?"

"Asked around."

"Have you found anyone who's been questioned?"

"No, but I haven't checked. Which is what I want to do now. If someone was asking, it means that the man who called at the Aldridge house can't have been a bent copper."

"Does it?"

"If he were, he'd have known, or could very easily have found out, who the eyewitness was. So is it all right if I start checking?"

"No."

"Why not?"

"Because you're talking a load of crap."

"It's logical . . ."

"Logic in a university is obviously very different from logic in the real world. According to you, in the car was the man who carried out a contract on Jenner and he reckoned he needed to skip the country fast because every copper in the country would be on the alert and Jenner's mob would either be celebrating or right behind the police. Right?"

68

"I know what you're going to say . . ."

"I'll still say it. If he was in such a bleeding hurry to get out of the country, why wasn't he driving through Clevestone the previous night?"

"I don't know, but there has to be a good reason."

"With your imagination, you can't think one up? Then I'll tell you what. He was shacked up with half a dozen blondes and it all took time." Frost started the engine and backed, seemingly careless whether or not he damaged his car by driving over Ballard.

They were having supper in the flat – two portions of Chicken Kiev from M & S and to come a small tub of Italian ice cream that was almost worth what it had cost.

Fleur looked across the folding table that was forever threatening to fold, which Ballard had bought at a boot sale. "You're very quiet. And last night you kept disappearing into a brown study. Something is wrong, isn't it?"

He shook his head.

"Yes, it is." She reached across to put a hand on his. "Remember our promise. No evasions. If something's bothering one of us, we talk it over, because openness is the secret of a relationship."

He laughed. "You've been reading that book again on how to have a secure marriage."

She jerked her hand away. "That's being very nasty. And very stupid if you think that what I said isn't true."

"It probably is, but I'd be more ready to accept the homily if the author hadn't just divorced his wife."

"How d'you know he has?"

"The news was in the paper a day or two ago."

"You didn't tell me you'd read that."

"I didn't want to undermine your faith."

"You really are a pig! . . . I can't think why I love you."

"It's my overwhelming charm."

"Will you let me sample that one day?" She reached across for his plate, piled it on top of hers, went through to the tiny kitchen. When she returned it was with two plates and the tub of ice cream. "Give me the smaller half because it's so rich that every spoonful adds inches."

"You can't have that."

"Why not?"

"There's no such thing as a smaller half; only a smaller portion."

"If you carry on like this, Geoffrey Ballard, I'll leave you for someone who wallows in split infinitives." She unscrewed the lid of the tub and tried to cut into the ice cream with a knife. "It's too hard for me to do." She passed tub, knife, and plates across the table. As he tried to force the knife down into the ice cream, she said: "Darling, is something wrong?"

"I suppose the refrigerator is turned up too high."

"Please don't go on being silly. I'm worried because you seem so distrait."

He decided to extract the ice cream in thick flakes rather than in halves. "Nothing's actually wrong, it's just . . ."

"Well?"

"You know how I think of the job?"

"Of course. There isn't one more important."

"Even if Joe Public equates importance with money. But we're the ones who allow the pop stars, the tennis champions, the footballers to earn their millions; without us, they'd just be singing or playing in the back streets. We're the thin blue line between civilisation and anarchy . . . Sorry, I'm on my soapbox again. Very boring." He picked up a plate and passed it across.

"Not boring, because I love hearing you talk like that. How many people in this materialistic age regard their job as a crusade?"

"Most have more sense."

"Don't start hiding your embarrassment behind cheap cynicism."

He pushed the empty tub to one side, picked up a spoon, but did not immediately eat. "It's sad. These days, we're not supposed to be proud to be British, to believe we're the best; in fact, we're not allowed to believe in anything much."

"Which is why it's all the more wonderful to hear you say what you've just said."

"Have I ever told you you're good for my ego?"

She giggled. "The book on marriage which you're so scornful about says that if each partner will worry more about the other's ego than his or her own the marriage will blossom like a datura."

"Does datura blossom excessively?"

"I've no idea."

"I'll bet the author didn't either, but it sounded good."

"Just stop being sarky and explain what's the problem that's biting you."

He ate a spoonful of ice cream. "It's like this . . ." He gave her a résumé of what had happened.

"Do you really think this man was a crooked policeman who was trying to persuade Aldridge he hadn't read the number correctly?"

"Most times there are one or two bent coppers around in the various forces and it's not difficult to see why – just for turning his eyes away from what they should be seeing, he can make as much as he'd earn in a year. But apart from being crooked, he's breaking his oath and every honest policeman hates his guts."

"You're saying you feel a personal need to find out the truth, aren't you?"

"I suppose so."

"But if Felix won't back you – because he's not the kind

71

of man to understand – what's to stop you having a word with Mr Lock?"

"He's closed the case down."

"But if you explained, I'm sure he'd see things your way. He's just as proud of being a policeman as you are."

He ate a couple more spoonfuls of ice cream.

"What are you thinking about now?" she asked.

"I was trying to gauge how Felix would react if he learned I'd gone over his head. He lives by the book and that means observing the chain of command."

"He'd huff and puff, but nothing more. He's burned out now, but I doubt he ever felt strongly about anything, even when young." She put her elbows on the table and rested her chin on the palms of her hands. "You're so different. If you believe, you act. Go and speak to Mr Lock and explain everything, just as you have to me. And if you so worried about upsetting Felix, why not see Mr Lock at his home, because then no one at the station will know anything about it. He'll be grateful, not annoyed, that you've spoken up."

Her enthusiasm convinced him.

Eleven

The Locks lived in south-east Staple Cross, in an area that was almost, but not quite, smart. Their house, built between the wars, was semi-detached, but large, and it boasted an elaborate porch that at the time had been considered smart, but was now generally regarded as pretentious. Ballard rang the bell. As he waited, he turned and stared at the garden, well illuminated by the nearby street lighting; obviously, someone was a keen gardener, but he found difficulty in picturing the detective inspector on hands and knees, weeding one of the rose beds . . . As the solid wooden door was opened to the length of a security chain, the sound caused him to turn back.

"Who is it?" a woman asked.

"Police Constable Ballard, Mrs Lock." Much safer not to promote himself to DC on this occasion. "I don't know if you remember that I was here quite recently when I brought some papers for the detective inspector and he was out? Is he in now?"

The door was closed, he heard the rasp of the chain being slid along the holder, then the door was opened fully. He said: "I'm sorry to bother you."

"I'm afraid Keith is not here."

"Then I'll call back another time."

"He will be back very soon, so why not come in and wait?"

Having nerved himself to speak to the DI, it would be an

anticlimax to turn away and leave, knowing he'd have to return another time. "Would you mind if I did that?"

"I'd welcome the company."

He entered the hall. Karen Lock was wearing a frock that in some subtle way, beyond his male competence to understand, drew attention to a figure so svelte it was difficult to believe she had had a child – which, he'd been told, had died in tragic circumstances. Gossip said she'd been a model before she married. That was easy to believe. Her wavy blonde hair framed an oval face notable for smooth symmetry and high cheekbones which added a touch of haughtiness.

She shut the door and secured the chain. "Let's go through to the sitting room."

He followed her. Many, perhaps even the majority, of the wives of senior officers cloaked themselves in their husbands' rank; she could hardly have been more friendly.

The sitting room was decorated in pastel colours and the furniture was of stripped pine; two medium-sized oil paintings, depicting seascapes, hung on one wall; the television was housed in a cabinet. It was a room of modern comfort, yet no particular character.

"What can I get you to drink?"

"Nothing, thanks."

"Last time it was difficult to persuade you to have a coffee, now you refuse a drink. Are you such an abstemious man in all departments?" Her tone was quiet amusement.

"I'll have to drive home," he said uncomfortably.

"And one drink will have you all over the road?"

"No, but . . ." He stopped.

"Perhaps you're worried that Keith would object to your drinking with me?"

"Nothing like that."

"Then you think he'd be perfectly happy?"

He was flustered, rapidly being drawn out of his depth. "It's just that . . . well . . ."

She laughed. "It's not fair to tease you, is it? Seriously, surely one small drink won't put you in danger of turning the breathalyser red, or whatever colour it goes? And it would be a kindness because I need a pick-me-up, but have the traditional reluctance to drink on my own."

What could he say but: "Then a lager would be very nice, Mrs Lock."

"We're assured on all sides that this is the age of Christian names. Mine is Karen. What's yours?"

"Geoffrey."

"Which means 'peace'. I'd say that that's very fitting. 'Karen' is said to derive from the Greek for pure. I naturally leave it to others to decide whether it suits me . . . I'll get the drinks." She left the room.

Did the mind rule the body or the body the mind? As she went through the doorway, he realised he'd been watching and had noticed how at each step her dress briefly tightened and outlined a buttock. Was this because he remembered what Ian had said about her and, without any conscious volition, was assessing the possibilities? If so, he was a fool. Her manner was merely more friendly than someone in the ranks might expect. And if one or two of the things she said might have had double meanings, that was because a man's mind, if primed, could find double meanings in a shopping order for bananas. If he'd had any sense, he'd have stuck to his refusal of a drink.

She returned, carrying a tray on which were two glasses. She crossed to where he sat and leaned over to hand him the tumbler. He tried not to look, but inevitably briefly looked. Swelling flesh was captured by a pink lace-edged brassière. As she went over to the settee, he was convinced she knew where his gaze had strayed, though had no idea why he should be certain.

She sat, crossed her legs and tugged her skirt down to cover a little more of her thighs.

A comment on her chaste character and rebuke for his licentious insolence, or a feminine ploy to draw attention to smooth, shapely thighs?

"You're obviously a man of few words, Geoffrey."

"I'm sorry."

"Very deep thoughts?"

"I'm afraid I was worrying about work."

"I call that the vice of the job, and like all vices, it causes endless trouble. We were supposed to be going out to dinner tonight, but at the last moment Keith said he couldn't make it because of work, which left me all dressed up and nowhere to go. I wish I had a pound for every time that's happened. I'd be a very rich woman. Interestingly, I've had wives ask me if I think their husbands really do work all the extra hours they claim to, or are they on the razzle. I never know what to answer. Tell me what I should."

"We do have to work long hours unexpectedly."

"That's a suspiciously ready answer. So share the secret, do you all agree to say the same thing so that when we wives get together, we've no cause for suspicion?"

"It's the truth."

"Are you married, Geoffrey?"

"Engaged."

"I've heard that described as the happiest of times as there's no past to cloud the present or the future. Tell me, and on my honour I promise never to divulge your answer, don't you occasionally join the lads around the bar and then, when you meet your fiancée long after you said you would, excuse yourself on the grounds that you suddenly had to rush off and question a witness?"

"I'm not obliged to say anything," he answered facetiously, trying by his answer to turn the question into a joke.

"An innocent man would have cried his innocence aloud; your guilt is obvious. 'Men were deceivers ever.'"

He could not resist briefly continuing the quote. "'One foot in sea, and one on shore, To one thing constant never.'"

"A copper who not only recognises but knows Shakespeare!"

"We're far from morons, Mrs Lock."

"But you do have short-lived memories. To remind you, my name is Karen. How quick you are to defend your companions. Wouldn't you agree that loyalty is the most noble virtue, disloyalty the most contemptible vice?"

He was disturbed by the sudden passion with which she had spoken; it was as if beneath her words lay some unusual emotion.

"Surely you don't have to plead the right of silence this time?"

"I suppose one could say something like that."

"Especially since your loyalty is self-evident. Your fiancée is a lucky lady to be engaged to you."

"Not as lucky as I am to be engaged to her."

"*Quelle politesse!*" She laughed.

He wondered if it was irony that had tinged her laughter or some other emotion.

The front door bell rang. "That will be Keith," she said. "I have to let him in because I always secure the chain to make certain I can't be interrupted."

'Interrupted'. Just an odd use of the word in the context? Or had she really been saying . . . Good God! he silently shouted. How mature did a man have to become before his mind no longer fantasised when in the company of an attractive, sexy woman?

Lock, followed by his wife, entered the room. "You want something?" he demanded, his tone sharply antagonistic.

Ballard hastily stood. "Yes, sir."

"What is it?"

It was all too obvious that he'd chosen a bad time to speak to the detective inspector. He wondered if there were some way he could put off the discussion, decided there was not.

"Whilst I'm waiting for an answer," Lock said to his wife, "perhaps you'd get me a gin and tonic so that our visitor doesn't suffer the embarrassment of drinking on his own."

"Stop being so grumpy," she replied. "For your information, he tried to refuse a drink because he's so very conscientious."

"But you obviously managed to bend his conscience."

"He was gentlemanly enough that in order to prevent my having to drink on my own he agreed."

As Karen left the room, Lock crossed to the second armchair and slumped down on it. Ballard hesitated, then sat.

"Well?" Lock demanded.

"I'm here, sir, to ask permission to pursue inquiries into the Clevestone hit-and-run."

"Why?"

"Because of the possibility that the man who called at Aldridge's place, and seems to have set out to confuse him, really was a policeman. There's the fact that the moment he realised Aldridge wore glasses for television he hammered home the point that Aldridge hadn't been wearing them when he tried to read the car's number, which had to mean he was very likely to have confused numbers and letters; it gave him a handle to breed in Aldridge's mind the belief that he was more likely than not to have made a mistake."

"There's only Aldridge's confused evidence to suggest any of that is what happened."

"But if it did—"

"If is not a word I like. CID is short-handed and crime is on an ever-upward spiral so since we cannot cover every incident as thoroughly as we would wish, I have to decide on priorities. The offence of not stopping after a traffic accident, even when fatal, when it is quite clear the driver was not at fault comes very low down; having to rely on an old man's evidence when he admits to a poor memory and has poor eyesight takes it down to zero."

"There's something else, sir."

"What?"

Karen entered and crossed to Lock's chair, handed him a glass. He thanked her curtly, then said: "You'd better find something to do elsewhere as this is work."

"I can always take a hint when it's delicately put," she said with sweet venom.

As she left the room, Ballard wondered why fate had been so unkind as to bring him to the house on an evening when husband and wife were at odds over a broken dinner date?

Lock drank, put the glass down on the occasional table by his side. "Am I to know what this something else is?"

"I started off by accepting Aldridge's evidence. I know, as you said a moment ago, he's old, has a poor memory and eyesight, but he's certainly not stupid or he'd never have thought to take the car's number or shout to his wife to note that down because—"

"Ballard, I've had a bloody heavy day and I've arrived home with enough work to keep me up into the early hours of the morning. So just avoid the obvious."

"Yes, sir. Accept Aldridge's evidence, and the question arises, why would anyone take the risk of trying to confuse his evidence? Surely, only if the accident could in some way be connected with a fairly major crime. I checked up on the various county crime lists and there was the Jenner shooting up north."

"Are you suggesting that in the car was the contract killer, on his way out of the country to avoid the manhunt following the shooting?"

"Yes."

"And he was in such a hurry that although the shooting took

place on the Thursday evening, he was not on the road until midday on the Friday?"

"I can't explain the delay, but there has to be an explanation."

"You sound like someone trying to put bones on the theory of quantum mechanics. Have you spoken to Sergeant Frost about your proposed theory?"

"Yes, I have."

"And he accepts your logic?"

"Like you, he reckons the gap in time seems to create a problem."

"He has always been a man who keeps both feet firmly on the ground. However, he saw sufficient merit in your ideas to suggest you spoke to me directly and as a matter of urgency – at my own home, if necessary?"

There was a long silence "Would I be wrong to conclude you are not here at Sergeant Frost's suggestion?"

"No, sir."

"Perhaps he dismissed the feasibility of your approaching me on the subject?"

Another silence.

"You surprise me. I had judged you to have the intelligence to realise that there is a chain of communication for a very good reason – it acts as a filter which shields senior officers from the more bizarre notions of their juniors."

"Sir, the trouble is the sergeant refuses to believe in the possibility of a bent copper."

"Unlike you, who finds no difficulty in doing so?"

"They have been known."

"Not in R Division."

"Isn't it being a little unrealistic to think—"

"As I said earlier, I have had a very tiring day."

"I'm sorry to go on and on . . ."

"Then don't."

Ballard stood. Then, despite the other's hostility, said: "Sir, may I have your permission to make inquiries in Clevestone to discover if anyone was trying to discover the identity of the eye-witness to the accident and also to check in Gransere if there's any trace of the green car and the people who were in it?"

"If you're not a complete fool, you'll know my answer."

Ballard left. As he opened the front door, Karen stepped into the hall from a short passage. "Good night, Mrs Lock," he said.

"Is it your memory or your nerve that's deficient?"

He went out and closed the door behind himself. As he walked toward his parked car, he wondered what her enigmatic smile had signified.

He drove into the yard at Ash Farm, turned off lights and engine, climbed out of the car. The moon was almost full and in its soft light the farmhouse, garden, land, and trees were invested with the quality of timeless peace.

Fleur met him at the front door and kissed him with enthusiasm, a clear indication that her parents, who led a social life, were out for the evening; had they been home, she would not have granted him more than a quick peck on the cheek, having been brought up to believe emotions were not for general display.

"Well?" she said. "Have you spoken to Mr Lock?"

"I've driven straight here from his place."

"Oh! From the sound of things, the meeting was difficult?"

"Make that bloody impossible."

"Come on through and tell me what happened."

They sat on the settee in the sitting room. She held his hand. "Wouldn't he listen to you?"

"Having suggested I'd more imagination than brains, he pointed out that there was a chain of communication to protect detective inspectors from the stupidities of police constables temporarily attached to CID."

"Couldn't he understand why you spoke to him after Felix had refused to take you seriously?"

"He didn't try. He was out when I arrived and Mrs Lock said to wait because he wouldn't be long. If I'd had any sense, I'd have said, 'Thanks, but no thanks.' When he turned up, he was as gritty as hell. They'd intended to go out for the evening, but he'd had to call everything off and it didn't need me to be a genius to guess she'd been giving him hell for upsetting the arrangement."

"You can't really blame her. It can be very annoying when all one's plans go for a burton."

"As you've mentioned once or twice! The trouble is, in busy times it can happen over and over again. Quite a few marriages end up on the rocks because of it."

She squeezed his hand. "Ours won't, will it?"

"Of course not." He spoke with absolute certainty. Their marriage would be far too secure to be blown off course by minor winds. "Mrs Lock seemed to be a bit of an oddball – she asked me whether I often stayed on after hours with the lads and then when I met you long after arranged said I'd been held up by work."

"Why did she ask that?"

"I don't really know."

"What was your answer?"

"You need to ask?"

"Of course."

"Never, never, never."

"With fingers firmly crossed?"

"Nasty!"

"Can't I tease you?" She reached up to nibble the lobe of his ear.

"That's becoming very teasing!"

She ceased nibbling. "It sounds as if he was bloody minded, but she was friendly?"

"Offered me a drink, and when I refused, went out of her way to make me change my mind."

"I bet she found that very difficult."

"As a matter of fact, she had to work hard . . . She became quite narked because I didn't call her by her Christian name."

"It's Claire, isn't it?'

"Karen. It's odd . . ." He became silent.

"What's odd about that? Your first girlfriend was Karen?"

"Annie, as far as I can remember; she was only six, but she wore lipstick and painted her nails a ghastly red, far too sophisticated for me. Mrs Lock made a point of telling me that Karen came from the Greek meaning 'pure', but she left it to other people to decide whether it suited her."

"Is that so strange?"

"If your name was Karen and you told me it meant pure, wouldn't you assume I'd be certain it suited you?"

"Knowing you, I'd be far more likely to expect you to hope it didn't."

"Be serious."

She laughed. "You mean, be generous."

"That wasn't the only thing. Once or twice she said something which had a double meaning."

"Being a woman, she probably had no idea it could have."

"I'm sure she knew very well."

"So you were all agog and hopeful?" She stood. "I'll get supper."

"Hang on. You can't really think it was like that," he protested. But from her expression, he gained the distinct impression that perhaps she could.

Twelve

The cafeteria could have been an understudy for a public lavatory with its tiled walls and air of stale humanity, but it was popular because it provided a place where tensions could be released, crudities exchanged, and superiors criticised with no risk of being overheard.

As Ballard crossed to the coffee dispensing machine he saw Ian Dean at one of the far tables, chatting up a blonde WPC whose name momentarily escaped him. He inserted a coin, waited, kicked the machine to prod it into life, held a plastic cup below the spout until it was full, went across.

"There's plenty of room elsewhere," Dean said.

Ballard sat.

"Here's a bloke who can't take a hint even when it's spelled out in capitals and underlined."

"Thank God some people can't read," she said.

Ballard remembered her name – Charmian. She had the salacious reputation of being a relief bicycle. The force remained a tough mark for women; if they tried to stand aside from the excesses, they were lessies, if they became one of the boys, they were ready marks. Canteen culture had a long way to go before it became politically correct.

Charmian pushed back her chair, stood.

"Be seeing you," Dean said.

"Not if I catch sight of you first." She walked away.

"She's got a pair of legs that could make a man give up

drink," he observed as he watched her thread her way between the tables to the exit doorway. He turned back. "I was making ground until you turned up."

"Confucius say, 'Pleasure delayed is pleasure replayed' . . . Do you remember mentioning what happened when you called at the Guv'nor's house and he wasn't there, but his missus was?"

"And if I do?"

"Tell me how things really went."

"Why?"

"I'm curious." Ballard drank some of the coffee, certain that Dean's resentment would be overcome by a desire to boost his own image.

Dean produced a pack of cigarettes, but did not bother to offer it. He struck a match. "You don't think it's the first time I've been given the sign, do you?"

"She's made willing before?"

"Not her. I'm talking generally. I'd need a computer to work out how often a woman's opened the front door of her place, taken one look at me, and smiled. I hadn't been in the force long enough to recognise a chief superintendent before I turned up at one place in my smart new uniform and knocked on the door and it was opened by a woman wearing a short nightdress . . ."

Ballard listened to a story which bore such similarity to the one Turner had told him a few days previously that a shared imagination seemed certain. "And the Guv'nor's wife met you in her nightie?"

"Not that time. But her dress did all the right things."

"And she was friendly?"

"The message was loud and clear."

"Did she ask you what your Christian name was?"

"Yeah. Which said everything, since most inspector's wives call you constable and couldn't care less whatever your surname is."

"Did she tell you what her Christian name was?"

"Asked me to call her Karen. Said her name meant pure and did I think it suited her. No shit! She was telling me to get cracking and find out."

"Which you did?"

"You think I keep my brains between my legs? She had the hots for me, but I wasn't going to risk burying my career ten feet deep by being caught shagging a DI's wife." He was silent for a moment. "Not that I haven't wondered more than once if the risk wouldn't have been worth it."

She'd asked them both to call her by her Christian name, Ballard thought, told them that Karen meant pure and did they think it suited her . . . Was it possible that the DI had been gritty not because she'd previously been giving him hell for breaking up their evening out, but because he'd found one of his hands in the house and was jealously certain what was going on?

Frost stepped inside the CID general room. "Where's Sam?"

"Not back, Sarge," Ballard answered. "He phoned through to say there's been some sort of cock-up, the case won't be over until the evening at the earliest, and prosecuting counsel says he must stay in court."

"And Tom?"

"I wouldn't know."

"Then get over to fourteen Alsop Street, Gransere, and take a statement from Mrs Livingstone regarding the mugging she witnessed in Oxford Street, London. Have you got that?"

Ballard wrote quickly on a loose sheet of paper. "All noted, Sarge."

"It seems she was too shocked at the time to say anything useful, but London's now hoping for a sharp description of the two men, so see what you can get out of her. And don't take the rest of the day doing it."

"I'll imitate Jehu."

"Who the hell's he?"

"The son of Nimshi, renowned for his furious chariot driving."

"It's a pity they didn't teach you something useful at university instead of a load of nonsense."

Edward the Seventh had visited Gransere several times for reasons never specifically detailed and this fact had given the seaside town an undeserved reputation which had survived. In truth, it had a stuffy character – the beach was pebble, the air too bracing for open-air amatory dalliance, and the council was very conservative. However, there was a large natural harbour and this had persuaded a company to build a marina with emphasis on quality; berthing rates were high and the yacht club, whose annual subscription was in the hundreds, offered accommodation where the staff never blinked when there was a generation gap between yacht owner and his 'wife'.

Mrs Livingstone had been more loquacious than helpful, despite Ballard's best efforts to persuade her to recall useful information, and he could be certain that Frost would consider he had failed. He left the house and settled in the CID Rover, was about to turn the key to start the engine when he checked his movements. Were he not to return to Staple Cross for another half-hour justice would not collapse; Frost would be unable to prove he had not left there as soon as he had finished interviewing Mrs Livingstone . . .

He drove down to the front, past several hotels larger than present-day trade warranted, to the marina, which enjoyed protection from bad weather to the east, north, and west, thanks to the curve of the bay. He parked beside an Aston Martin; on his walk, passed more large, luxurious cars than medium sized or family ones; to his right was an array of large yachts and motor cruisers. He pondered wealth, with the hope that before long fate would allow him to enjoy its paradoxes.

The harbour master's office was small and cluttered, the harbour master a fussy man with an egg-shaped face leathered by sun, wind, and rain, and a belly encouraged by a love of food and real ale. Having listened to Ballard he said: "Sorry, I can't help because I wasn't on duty that day. In the summer, the weekends are the busiest time so we work through 'em and then have time off during the week. Best have a word with my assistant, Reg Marr. He's checking out one of the water lines."

Ballard left the office and made his way to the western arm from which radiated six cross-arms; along the first of these, a man was kneeling by a tap. Ballard walked along the wooden slats, to the accompaniment of slapping noises, and as he approached, Marr looked up.

"Detective Constable Ballard, local CID. I'd like a word, if that's all right?"

"Fine by me, mate. This bloody tap's up the creek, I can't get the sodding thing off to see what's what, and the bloke who should be doing maintenance is off sick." Marr stood. Tall, a shade spindly, his face was badly marked from childhood acne. "So what's the problem?"

Ballard explained what he wanted to know.

"Friday between half twelve and one?" He scratched the back of his neck. "You're after a big green car with someone in it what looked like he was in a hurry to get to sea . . ." He shook his head. "We're always busy because there's something needs sorting out; blokes with money like to show how grand they are and have the biggest boat they can afford, but most of 'em have as much common sense as a newt and never stop screwing things up."

"The car was probably showing signs of recent damage at the front; maybe a bent wing."

Marr brought a pack of cigarettes out of his boiler suit pocket. "D'you use these?"

"Thanks, but I don't."

"My girlfriend keeps on at me to give 'em up; says it just needs will-power. I tell her, I've plenty of that, but I've better things to use it on. Nothing's that easy, anyway. Particularly this sodding thing." He looked resentfully down at the tap before he struck a match. The breeze was so light that the smoke from the cigarette rose several inches before it began to be shuffled sideways. "A bent wing . . . I do remember something. There was a car . . ." He became silent.

"Tell me about it."

"A green S-class Mercedes, good as brand new. Had a buckled wing what looked as if it had been rubbing on the tyre. Turned up just before I had me lunch."

Ballard experienced a rising excitement. "Where were you when you saw it?"

"Down by the light crane, talking to Mr Tubb – great name for a bloke who looks like a billiard ball. Has hotels all over the country, so they say, and owns that one with the blue hull." Marr pointed to a large motor cruiser moored bows-in along the next marina arm. "Twin turbo diesels and she'll make twenty knots if pushed; cruises at fifteen."

"You were talking to him when this car drove up," Ballard prompted. "So who was in the car?"

"There was two blokes. And looking at one of 'em, I said to myself, 'I'll not argue the toss with you, mate. If you say the Earth's flat, flat it is.'"

"You're saying he was a hard case?"

"But not a thug. Far from it. Smartly dressed. But the way he moved around and his expression which said he wasn't stepping aside for anyone . . . Tough."

"Did either man go on to a yacht?"

"The second one boarded, yeah."

"But not the first as well?"

"He returned to the car and drove off."

"Can you describe the second man?"

Marr tried to do so.

"You can't do better than that?"

"It's difficult enough with someone who looks like someone, but he looked like no one. I mean, five seconds after seeing him, he was just a blur in the memory. Come to that, he was just a blur when I was looking at him."

"Was he met by someone from the yacht?"

"No. Just went up the gangplank and disappeared into the accommodation."

"Was he carrying anything?"

"A couple of cases."

"Suitcases?"

"I suppose that's what they was, only they wasn't the usual kind of shape. Like as not, made by one of those arty-farty firms what charge three times as much for their name."

"Tell me what kind of shape they were."

"They was long and thin instead of being kind of square."

One could have been a gun case, the other a match in order to divert possible suspicion. "How soon after he went on the yacht did it leave?"

"She, mate, not it. Boats are always shes. Know why? The more screws they have, the faster they move . . . She sailed near enough straight away."

"Was it – she – a big boat?"

"An eighty-foot yawl – good for any sea, not like them gin palaces." He jerked his head in the direction of several motor cruisers, all with high superstructures. "One of them meets a force eight wind and she's kaput. This yawl, with almost no deckhead above the deck line, could ride a force twelve if the skipper knows his job. And she was as shipshape as you'll see. Hull painted a deep blue, brass polished, rigging new, varnish fresh . . . You don't see many that smart with the cost of maintenance what it is today."

"Did you note her name?"

"Never bothered to look. She flew the Spanish flag, that's all I can say."

"Will there be a record of what her name is?"

"Depends if she was tied up for more'n twenty-four hours."

"Will the harbour master be able to tell me whether she was?"

"If he can find the energy to look in the log."

"You're being a great help."

"Then return the favour and tell me how to free this sodding tap."

"Call a plumber."

Marr did not find that amusing.

"One last thing. I don't suppose there's any chance you noted all or any part of the registration number of the green Mercedes?"

"ANE," was the immediate reply.

Ballard's voice expressed his surprise. "You're certain?"

"The girlfriend's names are Annie Nell Edwards. Seeing them letters, I thought how I'd like to give her a personalised number plate with a Mercedes to go with it."

"What about the numbers?"

Marr shook his head.

Ballard thanked him and left. As he walked back to the harbour master's office, he decided, with a degree of immodest self-congratulation, that it was looking more and more as if his imaginative reconstruction of events was correct.

The harbour master was eating chocolate sponge cake; by the side of the plate was a mug of instant coffee.

"Sorry to bother you again," Ballard said, "but your assistant's told me something interesting and I need to try to check things further."

The harbour master nodded as he used a fork to slice off a

91

piece of cake. "Having a bit of a snack to see me through until supper."

'A bit of a snack' was at least two normal portions, Ballard estimated. "According to him, a Spanish yacht was in harbour last Friday midday when it picked someone up from shore, and I'd like to know its name. Is there any chance of your being able to tell me what that is?"

The harbour master chewed, swallowed. "Depends. If a yacht comes in and just waters or fuels and is only a few hours alongside, we don't bother to take details and log 'em."

"Would you check if this yacht was in long enough to be logged?"

He put another mouthful of cake into his mouth and chewed contentedly as he crossed to a chart table under which were drawers; from one of these he brought out a large ledger-style book. He laid this down on the table. "Last Friday?"

"That's the day."

He opened the book, turned a couple of pages, ran finger down the entries. "No."

"She wasn't here Thursday night?"

"That's right."

But if his theory was correct, she should have been waiting for the hit man – who had not turned up until the Friday . . .

The harbour master returned to his seat and another piece of cake. Through a mouthful, he said: "There was a foreign yacht came in Thursday evening for water and when I asked to see the papers they said they'd be leaving before midnight. That's what she must have done because she wasn't here in the morning when I checked. Some of the foreigners try a fast one to avoid the dues and I have to keep my eyes open. Which ain't to say the British are any way behind in trying. But they have to be smart to fool me!"

"I'm sure they do." He'd not learned very much, Ballard thought, but what he had was going to cause a stir.

Thirteen

"It all fits," Ballard said, as he stood in front of the detective sergeant's desk.

Frost leaned back in his chair.

"An S-class green Mercedes – a big car in anybody's vocabulary. It showed signs of damage to a front wing and arrived at the marina close to one o'clock which is what it would have done had it been just beyond Clevestone at twelve seventeen. The man who boarded the yacht was carrying two unusually shaped suitcases – one of them could have had a stripped down rifle inside. The yacht sails as soon as he's aboard . . . He was the contract killer, getting out of the country by a safe route."

"And in such a hurry to escape that he didn't bother to arrive at the marina until after midday on the Friday?"

"Previously when you made this point, I said something must have turned up to change the timetable. There's proof this happened in the fact the yacht was in the marina the previous evening, sailed out when those aboard discovered it would be logged if they stayed the night, returned to pick up a man at around one in the afternoon on the Friday."

"You call that proof?"

"Yes."

"Maybe words have different meanings when you know so many of 'em . . . Have you stopped to think about the description of the bloke who went on to the yacht?"

"Marr wasn't really able to describe him."

"Precisely. It's a good guess that he's the kind of bloke who looks in a mirror and doesn't see anyone."

"If you're suggesting he's too weak to be a hit man, one doesn't need to be a Hercules to fire a rifle."

"To pull the trigger, no; to pull it knowing you're killing someone and that from the moment you do you're on the run, that needs loads of bottle."

"So his looks don't live up to his abilities. And could you think up a better camouflage? I've checked the three letters Marr gave me . . ."

"Without permission?"

"Sarge, this is turning out to be a murder inquiry."

"Makes no difference."

Trust Frost to rate rules above results! "The letters show the car was registered in Manchester. It's reckoned Jenner was killed because of arguments over drug territory and Manchester is close to where he was operating."

Frost picked up a pencil and began to roll it between thumb and forefinger. "Marr could have got the letters wrong."

"Not this time. They're the initials of his girlfriend; you don't make a mistake over them."

"Depends how often you change girlfriends."

"And they tell us something more, don't they? Aldridge only got one letter wrong, so his eyesight's not as bad as people have been assuming. His figures could be right, or only those easily confused could be wrong. I've visually checked with those he's given – writing them out and looking at them at a distance – and I reckon that only two of them might easily be mistaken, the five and the eight."

"So?"

"We check out permutations with the correct letters."

"All this in a case that's dead?"

"The Guv'nor's got to bring it back to life."

94

Frost sighed. "You know the worst cross a sergeant has to bear? Someone who confuses initiative with making waves."

Friday brought a sharp change of weather. Gone were the blue skies and bright sunshine, to be replaced by total cloud coverage and a sharp wind from the west. Summer had returned.

Fleur had wanted to borrow Ballard's car – her parents had been going out for the day and she had been invited to a hen party after she finished her half-day's work – and so he caught a bus which dropped him two roads from divisional HQ. He walked briskly, his thoughts cheerful. Frost's response to his ideas the previous day had been deprecating, but anyone less sourly dismissive would have to appreciate the value of his work. He surely must have earned himself a commendation on his flimsy, as the confidential reports on suitability for promotion were known . . .

When he entered the detective sergeant's room, the tone of his greeting matched his mood. "Morning, skipper."

"If you say so."

"Has the OK been given to check out the registration numbers and identify the owners?"

"No."

"What? You've got to be joking!"

"I don't make a habit of joking," snapped Frost, oblivious to the reverse humour of his reply.

"Then what's going on?"

"I'll tell you exactly what's going on. If I try to push my luck any harder with the Guv'nor he swears he'll have me back in uniform, working myself into an early grave as custody sergeant."

"But didn't you explain that now we're not dealing just with a car that didn't stop, it's the Jenner murder?"

"Yes."

"What did he say to that?"

"If he had your imagination, he'd take up astrology."

"The facts fit."

"Like a screwdriver fits a nut."

"You've got to persuade him he's being totally short-sighted."

"You think inspectors are in the habit of being told they're fools by their sergeants? I'd tell you who's being a fool, only I don't reckon you've the equipment to understand. There's a pile of bumph on your desk that needs checking and typing. Go do it."

He left and went along the corridor to the CID general room, sat at his desk and stared at the heap of papers on it. Black thoughts returned . . . For a time it had been reasonable to accept the DI was justified in halting inquiries into the accident which had killed Simon Kerr; the case had a very low priority and the chances of identifying the car had appeared to be virtually nil. But now, when it was probable the car had been carrying the contract killer, it seemed there could be only one reason for the DI's refusing to follow the lead he had been given . . .

It was a conclusion he still fought against. Strictly speaking, there was not a scrap of proof that the Mercedes which arrived at the marina had been involved in the accident near Clevestone, that the man who had boarded the yacht had murdered Jenner; it was assumptions, coincidences, imagination, that linked the events and the persons to those events. Lock's reputation named him as straight and honest as any man could be and there were no better judges of character than working companions . . . Yet reputation could be assiduously cultivated, the truth carefully concealed. If his theory was correct, the hit man enjoyed the near perfect camouflage of appearing to be a nobody. Wasn't dedicated honesty an equally effective veil?

He hoped he was wrong. Because if Lock was bent, justice became a sick joke.

*   *   *

It was three-quarters of an hour after he had returned to his flat before Fleur arrived in his car.

She kissed him. "Sorry I'm late." She kissed him again. "Dorothy turned up late in the day and kept us all in stitches describing life with her third husband. I lost track of time. Forgive?"

"I don't know."

She kissed him yet again. "And now?"

"I'm still not certain."

"Well, I am certain you're being too greedy."

They went through to the sitting/dining room and she settled in the one armchair. "You're looking tired, my darling. Has work been worse than usual?"

He didn't answer the question. "What will you drink? Cinzano, gin, or lager?"

"Cinzano and soda, please."

He walked around the dining table, one leg of which had to be propped up because it had been broken and then repaired badly, to the cupboard in which he kept the drink. He poured out two Cinzanos, added soda. "Ice?"

"Don't bother; it's not very warm today."

Her tone had said, "Yes, please." He went into the tiny kitchen and brought the ice tray out of the refrigerator, dropped a cube into each glass. Back in the other room, he settled on the settee, raised his glass. "The first today and all the sweeter for it."

She told him the Mountforts had spoken to her parents; they were now wondering whether they would in fact offer the tenant a fresh lease if he did decide he wanted to stay on in their cottage.

"If you ask me, we can forget the idea of buying that place."

"Why d'you say that?"

"They obviously can't make up their minds. They can go on

saying yes and no from now until the next millennium and leave us homeless."

"Father says they're always like this, but he has great hopes they will soon decide."

"I wish I were half as optimistic."

"And I wish you were too. What is the matter? Are you very annoyed because I was late?"

"I was worried."

"But I'm here now, so you can stop remembering and cheer up."

He tried to do so, but it soon became obvious he'd failed.

"Geoff, you've got to tell me what the trouble is. Have I done or said something to annoy you?"

"It's nothing whatsoever to do with you. It's work. Something's happened and I don't know what to do because I may be making a total burk of myself."

"Can you tell me or is it top secret?"

"I can't stop wondering . . . I think it's just possible . . . What would you say if I told you I suspected the detective inspector is bent?"

She had lifted her glass to drink, now held it steady and stared at him over the rim. "Are you being serious?"

"Yes. And I wish to God I weren't."

"But you've always said he's the straightest person you've met in the force; that he can be hard, but that can't really be resented because he's always just."

"I'd have staked everything on that."

"Then what on earth's happened to make you change your ideas?"

He explained.

She fiddled with a button on the front of her dress. "You say you can't really prove a thing."

"But when facts fit in so smoothly, it seems like proof. All right, I may be making a fool of myself; like I've just said, I hope I am. But someone called on Aldridge and claimed to be a policeman, but didn't give his name, then worked hard to make certain Aldridge's evidence became virtually useless. And the DI's blocked everything I've tried to do. Now there's reason to think there could be a direct connection between the accident and the murder and he's still blocking when one would have expected him to check every possibility."

"Have you spoken to Felix about your suspicions?"

"Not directly."

"Wouldn't that be a good idea?"

"Probably not. The idea would appal him and he'd refuse to give it the slightest credence."

"Then you have to decide on your own where you go from here."

"Easy to say. Bloody difficult to do."

"I know that. But I also know you'll do it."

"Will I?"

"Of course, because you're the kind of person you are."

"The easiest and safest course is to forget everything."

"Knowing there's the possibility the person in charge of CID may be corrupt?"

"Knowing that I will be saving my job. It's a sacking offence under the Code of Discipline to make a serious false accusation against a fellow policeman."

"Darling, you do know my parents weren't all that pleased when I said I was going to marry you, don't you?"

"Their careful politeness said it all."

"They changed their minds and now couldn't be more happy about the marriage because they realised you're someone who honours standards, believes in justice, hates any sort of wrong because it hurts the innocent."

"You're saying I have to go ahead and find out the truth, aren't you?"

"If you're not to let yourself down."

*　　*　　*

The politicians had always been the police's enemy. There were headlines to be gained from appeasing do-gooders, quoting tired old aphorisms about guilt and innocence, crying foul when a policeman had to use force to defend himself from a vicious attack, calling for better efficiency while demanding a cut in the cost of the service . . .

The police had direct computer access to vehicle identification, but because they were using a service set up by another government body, they were charged for every inquiry. Singly, the amount in question was minimal, but by the end of an accounting quarter the total could become considerable. Because of this, the order in the county force was that except in the case of 'hot need' (e.g. the crew of a patrol car wanting to know the name of the registered owner of a car they were following), permission had to be sought before a request for identification was made.

On Monday morning, Ballard asked one of the civilian workers at the station to put forward the registration numbers he gave her and named the detective inspector as authorising officer. The higher the rank, the less likely the request would be queried.

Fourteen

The internal phone in the CID room rang and White, his growing beard black enough to cause many weak jokes, answered it. After replacing the receiver, he called across the room: "Geoff, communications have a message for you."

Ballard left and went down three floors to the communications centre, manned by both uniform and civilian staff. A middle-aged woman with buck teeth, cruelly known as Rabbit, handed him a sheet of paper on which had been printed several names and addresses.

Since the Mercedes's registration number had been allotted to Manchester, it was reasonable to suppose the car had been bought by someone who lived in that area. He faxed the list of names to the Greater Manchester, West Yorkshire, South Yorkshire, Derbyshire, Staffordshire, and Cheshire county forces, asked if any of the people listed had a criminal record and, if so, for a copy of that record. He could have contacted Central Records, but by restricting inquiries to the local forces there was less likelihood of any damaging feedback.

Requests to other forces usually took a long time to be dealt with – other people's problems were never as pressing as one's own – but by early Wednesday morning, as Ballard was about to leave the station, the penultimate answer arrived from the Cheshire force. He read: 'No name has a criminal record' with an inward sigh of relief. Five down, one to go.

101

Hopefully, he would soon be certain that his theory had been the result of an imagination out of control . . .

As he put the paper in the right-hand drawer of his desk, the detective inspector stepped into the general room. "Ballard."

"Sir?"

"In my room, now." The DI turned, left.

Turner said: "If you ask me, sport, you're in for a right old bollocking!"

The Germans had a word for it, Ballard thought. *Schadenfreude*. Turner was on night duty, so there was a degree of pleasure to be gained from seeing someone about to go off duty in trouble.

He entered the DI's room.

"Close the door."

He shut it, crossed the floor to stand in front of the desk.

"Are you incapable of obeying orders?"

He was uneasily disturbed by the anger in the other's voice – Lock was normally in full control of his emotions. "What particular order are you referring to, sir?"

"Have you disobeyed so many that you can't identify any particular one?" Lock went over to the window and stared out at the road for several seconds, then turned back. "I run the CID with as light a hand as possible because I consider that the best way; if a man has sufficient intelligence and initiative to be here, there should be no need to watch every move he makes. You are gaining experience under the special entry scheme, and I had assumed there would be no need to treat you any differently. I obviously made a mistake."

"I still don't understand, sir."

"I've just had reason to speak to the DCI of the West Yorkshire force and in the course of the conversation he mentioned that the list of names we had sent them had been checked and none of them had criminal records – a fax to that effect had been sent a while back to DC Ballard. I could have asked him what he was talking about since I'd no idea, but that would have made me look a bit of a fool." He walked to the desk, but did not sit. "Would you care to explain now so that I'm no longer all at sea?"

"I wanted to know if any of the names had a record, sir."

"Where do the names come from?"

"They were provided by vehicle identification."

"Except in 'hot' circumstances, either Sergeant Frost or I have to give authority for a search request to be made. Since in this instance I did not give any such authority, would I be correct to presume that Sergeant Frost did so?"

"No, sir."

"No?"

"I . . . I used your name, sir."

"Really! Would you not call that a form of forgery?"

"I was so certain I'm right, I had to find out the facts one way or the other."

"You find it reasonable to use a lie to seek the truth? A strange proposition for a policeman. What truth were you seeking?"

"Whether the man who shot Jenner was in the car which hit and killed Simon Kerr."

"Are you a fool?"

"I don't think so, sir."

"Then did Sergeant Frost forget to tell you that it was my decision no further action in the Simon Kerr case was to be taken?"

"He told me that, sir."

"So you chose to ignore my orders?"

"In a way, but—"

"Is it your contention that a PC, temporarily attached to CID, is entitled to question a decision made by his detective inspector, and if he decides on such a course, to ignore it?"

"I couldn't understand why you originally made the order; and then why you wouldn't check out whether the killer of Jenner could have been in the car that ran over Simon Kerr."

Lock's voice sharpened still further. "But clearly you envisaged a possible reason since you ignored my order to the extent of forging my name. Would you like to explain what that reason was?"

"It's almost certainly a complete nonsense, sir."

"You would rather not spell it out? Why? Because you think I might find it insulting?"

Ballard was silent.

Lock sat. "The circumstances being what they are, I shall request your transfer back to uniform duties."

"Why?"

"You really need to ask?"

"I was trying to get to the truth. That's supposed to be our job."

"Suffering so unstable an imagination, I question your ability to recognise what truth is. That's all."

Fleur looked at Ballard across the restaurant table. "Have you forgotten that this is meant to be celebrating the anniversary of when we first met?"

The waiter appeared with a bottle of Chilean red wine, showed it to Ballard, opened it with professional ease and poured a taste into Ballard's glass. Ballard smelled it as custom dictated, even though he wasn't certain he would know a sick Chilean red from a Château Margaux by smell alone, tasted it. He nodded. The waiter filled their glasses, left. He fiddled with the stem of the glass. "I was hauled into the DI's room just before I left the station because he'd learned I'd been making inquiries after he'd given the order to close the case down."

"Oh, dear! Was it rough?"

"Extra rough because he didn't have to be told I'd begun to suspect him."

"Couldn't he understand?"

"A detective inspector who learns that a PC seconded to his CID is wondering if he's turned crooked is unlikely to be in an understanding mood."

"But surely you've never openly accused him?"

"Of course not."

"Then how can he do anything about it?"

"By having me transferred back to the uniform branch."

"How serious will that be?"

"It'll put the kybosh on my gaining accelerated promotion; it might even have more drastic consequences."

"If you've never spoken openly, he can only guess at what you've suspected."

"True, but that's not what will officially be at issue. He'll get me for falsely using his name to authorise the request for vehicle identification. He'll call it forgery."

"I'll bet you're not the first to do something like that."

"Or the last. My sin is to be caught doing it."

"He'll have done the same sort of thing in the past. Surely he won't damn you just because of that?"

"It'll be the window dressing. The real reason why he's going to kick me out is because I dared suspect him."

"That's being totally small-minded."

"He's a proud man."

"Explain that what you were truly doing was trying to prove the impossibility of his being a traitor."

"But I've thought that's just what he might be."

"For goodness' sake, stop being so hopelessly pedantic."

He smiled briefly.

"That's better!" She sipped the wine, replaced the glass on the table. "You know, I'm glad you're certain you were wrong about him. I've always thought him the epitome of what a policeman should be."

"I can't be certain quite yet. There's still the report to come through from Derbyshire."

"Have you reason for thinking it'll be any different from the others?"

"No."

"Then it won't be."

A waiter brought the Serano ham and melon that each was having. She waited until he left, then said: "Mr Lock is a sensible man, so if you explain carefully, he'll understand that what you did was right because you were looking for the truth."

Women, he thought, were ruled by emotion; the emotion of their desire. For his money, the DI would not be in the least understanding.

On his desk in the general room next morning was a two-page fax from the Derbyshire police. He began to read, his mind half on the words, half on trying to decide whether he should follow Fleur's suggestion and speak to Lock and explain that what had driven him had been a regard for the honour of the force . . .

Abruptly, his mind was wholly on what he was reading. David Cairns. Two convictions for juvenile crime when in his very early teens; a conviction for assault causing grievous bodily harm when twenty-two; an extract from a 'khaki book' (known facts which could not be proved in a court of law, suspicions, and rumours) – he had worked as enforcer for a mob that had disbanded after two of the top guys had ben wasted by rivals; subsequently, the mob had been reactivated by Edwin Hastings. Hastings, with rare brutality, had carved out a territory in which his mob ran all the usual rackets, including drugs, prostitution, and protection. Cairns, a smart operator, had become Hastings's lieutenant; when Hastings had suffered health problems and stepped down from active management, he had taken over direct control. Hastings's present whereabouts was not known, but he was rumoured to be abroad, in Spain; whilst no longer in hands-on command, his authority even at a distance was sufficient that what he said, was. The mob was run with skill, and thanks to the advice of crooked lawyers it had proved impossible to bring to court Cairns or any other of the higher-ups. Over the past months, the major threat to the mob had not been the police, but another outfit run by Robert Jenner, who was intent on taking over the territory. There had been several violent clashes, in which four had been severely wounded, but arrests had been impossible because of the usual lack of evidence. Very recently, there had been the murder of Jenner. Rumour said he had been shot by an imported hit man, sent in by Hastings. Cairns and several others had been questioned to no effect; all had perfect alibis for the time of the murder – a fact which underlined their guilt.

The message ended with a request for any information which came to hand that might assist inquiries into the murder of Jenner.

Eureka! Ballard silently shouted, enjoying the sweet smell of success after suffering the sour smell of failure. A dogged pursuit of the truth had finally reached it because even the smartest of men made mistakes. Cairns's had been not to use a stolen car to drive the hit man to the boat. But how could he have foreseen this would matter when there could be no suspicion attached to his car's being on the road on the Friday unless it was in a fatal accident because a boy would lose control of a motor scooter and end up under the front wheels?

Ballard's sense of triumph waned. This new evidence virtually confirmed that the man who had questioned Aldridge on the evening of the accident had been a genuine policeman; that his aim had been to scramble Aldridge's memory. The finger once more pointed directly at the detective inspector . . .

He left and went along to the detective sergeant's room.

Frost's greeting was to the point. "You're a bloody fool!"

"What makes you say that?"

"If you don't know, you're an even bigger one than I thought. Why the hell did you go on rummaging around when the order was to close down the case?"

"I've tried to explain."

"You still have a head filled with thoughts of saving the world from catastrophe?"

"Just the little bit I can see."

"If they're all like you at university, I'd shut every bloody one in the country and save a fortune." His voice rose. "I've suffered ten minutes in the DI's room, being roasted. I tried to say that if we're sent someone as goddamn stupid as you, nothing's going to run smooth, but he wouldn't listen. If I get bollocked, I like it to be because it's me what's done something stupid, not because some plod's so thick that he's flatly disobeyed orders. When you were born, they must've stuffed feathers between your ears, not brains. You know what the DI said to me? That you were accusing him of being crook. Jesus! A PC comes into CID and tells the DI he's bent!"

"I didn't put it into words."

"You think he's as way-out dim as you are? He knew what you weren't saying out loud because you hadn't the guts. He's going to request your transfer back to uniform and I'll endorse that twice over. And if uniform have any sense, they'll suggest you take perpetual leave before you start shouting the chief constable is a paedophile."

Ballard put the fax down on the desk.

"What's that?"

"I sent five police forces a list of names—"

"Names you obtained by faking the DI's signature."

"What else was I to do when he wouldn't follow up the evidence?"

"You still don't understand, do you?"

"Sarge, it's you who don't. Read the fax."

Frost reluctantly picked up the paper and read. When he put it down, his expression suggested severe dyspepsia. "I wish to God I'd woken up with appendicitis and been carted off to hospital," he muttered.

Fifteen

L ock, working at his desk, looked up. "Yes?"
Frost entered the office, his reluctance obvious; Ballard
followed him. "I'd like a word, sir."

"I have a very busy morning."

"Yes, sir, but . . . Well . . ."

Lock stared past Frost at Ballard. "I very much doubt
there's anything can be usefully said." There were times
when the lines in his face tightened to add hardness, perhaps
even a touch of viciousness, to his features.

"I think, sir, you should . . . ?"

"I am not in the habit of being told by my sergeant what I
should or shouldn't do. And I suggest that you consider the
fact that whilst a sense of loyalty towards the members of
one's team is admirable, there are times when it becomes
completely misplaced."

The other's misunderstanding of the purpose of this visit
compounded Frost's nervousness. "It's . . . What I . . ."

Ballard said: "Sir, would you read the fax from Derbyshire." He took the fax from Frost and stepped forward to
put it on the desk.

"Is this to do with the list of names you have been sending
out without my authorisation?"

"Yes, sir."

He picked up the fax, read. As often happened in moments
of mental tension, Ballard's mind drifted as a way of relieving

110

that tension. Frost looked like a rabbit being stalked by a stoat. When young, Ballard had gone for a walk with his mother along lanes through the countryside and a sudden and prolonged screaming had frightened and sickened him. She had made him follow her into the copse which bordered the lane and there they had disturbed a stoat which had attacked a rabbit, too mesmerised to have tried to escape. He had tried to revive the rabbit, but it had died in his hands. When he'd cried, his mother had told him he was old enough to understand that when the world appeared most beautiful, cruelty lurked as closely as ever. At the time, he had not realised she might have been thinking of her husband, not the stoat . . .

"This has just been received?" Lock asked.

Ballard waited for Frost to answer, but it seemed the other had mentally disassociated himself from a situation he could not handle. "Yes, sir. I showed it to Sergeant Frost, then we brought it here."

"For once observing the lines of communication?"

Ballard had wondered how the detective inspector would react; he had not expected calm irony.

"Clearly, I should have remembered my first sergeant, who would have been totally out of place in the modern force, yet was one of the sharpest coppers I've served with. He maintained that if you reached the right conclusion, it didn't matter what route you took. By his standards, your disobedience of orders and forgery of my name have become immaterial. No doubt you would agree . . . Presumably, you see this information as confirmation of all you've been suggesting?"

"Yes, sir."

"And thinking?"

"I . . . ?"

"Perhaps we should move on. I presume you realise that despite this there is still no hard proof your theory is correct.

And you'll accept that coincidence has long arms and one of them might well have been stretched out here?"

"It shouldn't be difficult to find out if that's the case. If Cairns's Mercedes shows signs of recent damage, we'll be able to say one coincidence too far."

"I wonder if defence counsel would accept that? However, they are notoriously small-minded . . . Very well. I'll get in touch with Derbyshire and suggest they conduct a thorough examination of the car. I presume the motor scooter is still with Vehicles?"

Frost, faced with a question that did not take him into realms he feared, answered: "They won't have returned it yet, sir."

"Tell them to go over it again for contact evidence, however thoroughly they claim to have already done so, and then to forward any details to you for passing on to Derbyshire . . . Of course, even if the car shows damage from the scooter, there's no evidence that the contract man was in it. But that'll be their problem; we'll have cleared up our hit-and-run. Is there anything more you suggest we do?"

"No, sir."

"That's all, then."

They turned and began to cross to the doorway, came to a halt when Lock said: "Ballard. Good work!"

"Thank you, sir."

They left. Ballard was about to carry on past the detective sergeant's room when Frost, who'd entered, called him inside. Frost went round the desk and sat. "Have you learned something?"

"I think so, Sarge."

"I bloody well hope so. You realise, don't you, that there aren't many in his position would have turned round and praised you?"

"But I did get things right . . ."

112

"You're still trying to say he's crook?"

"Of course I'm not when he makes a point of reopening the investigation. I meant, the other things I said."

"To him, the rest wouldn't count. You hit his pride. God knows how you could've been so daft. I tell you, if you can't read people better than you've read him, you'll never be any good at this job."

"I know it sounds stupid now, but it was the way things looked."

"It's the way you look at evidence that counts, not the way it looks at you."

"But it did seem odd – to some extent still does . . ."

"I'm beginning to think you've learned SFA," Frost said angrily.

"I guess I'm just reluctant to admit I've made a pig's arse of everything."

"No need to admit that. It's bloody obvious."

Fleur and Ballard had been invited to supper with newly married friends of hers and he drove into the yard at Ash Farm at ten past eight. As he climbed out of the car, Fleur came round the corner of the house, opened the garden gate, and hurried towards him. He was about to kiss her decorously on the cheek when she side-stepped him. "There's no time for that." She went round the bonnet of the car and settled on the front passenger seat. He started the engine, backed, drove up to the gateway where he stopped for an oncoming car.

"Why the crashing silence? Are you in a very grumpy mood?"

"Just wondering why you have such different priorities to me."

"You're sulking because I wouldn't kiss you hullo? I hate being late and reckoned we could make up for it later on."

"In that case, maybe I'll accept your apology."

"I didn't make one; I was offering consolation. I'm in a rush because you've already held us up twenty minutes."

"I couldn't help that."

"The thing is, we're the first non-family Nancy's had to a meal since returning from the honeymoon, so she's cooking something special. She told me that if you hold things up and everything's burned or dries out, she'll either collapse or murder you."

"Faced with the alternative, I'd rather she collapsed."

"How very noble! But at least you're smiling again."

"At the thought of my consolation, not her fate."

"Men really do have one-track minds."

"Why not, when all roads lead to nirvana."

"I thought one only reached there after extinction of all desires?"

"Then for nirvana, read heaven."

"Instead of talking nonsense, tell me what sort of a day you've had."

"Very odd."

"Explain."

He slowed for crossroads, checked they were clear, drew out to the right. As they drove along a road that was dappled with the shadows of hedgerow trees by the sinking sun, he explained the course of events.

She said, when he'd finished speaking: "Mr Lock didn't hold things against you, then?"

"Obviously not. And as I was leaving, he even said, 'Good work.' From him, that's high commendation."

"Did you apologise?"

"What for?"

"Reckoning he could be crooked, of course."

"Since I never accused him, it didn't seem necessary."

"It would still have been a nice thing to do."

"I'm far from certain about that. When nothing's said, both sides can imagine it was never thought."

"That's a bit of warped thinking! You know, love, I still can't understand how you can have begun to think he was crooked."

"He kept blocking any inquiry into the facts."

"You've told me more than once that the police can never cope properly with all crime and have to work to priorities. Surely that's what he was doing?"

"When it seemed a bent copper might be involved, I'd have expected him to pull out all the stops."

"He obviously didn't think it nearly as possible as you did."

"He should have done."

She laughed.

"I'm not saying I'm omniscient."

"You could have fooled me."

"All right, maybe I do occasionally sound too certain of myself, but I . . . If the honour of the force is queried, I reckon the problem has to become priority number one."

She briefly touched his left arm. "And so you should. Just teasing you. So even if he hasn't done what you thought he should, you don't have any more doubts about him?"

"None at all. But there is still a niggle. Who was the man who deliberately tried to scramble Aldridge's memory?"

"Didn't you once say he might have been a journalist?"

"It was a suggestion. A check with local and national papers would soon find out if that were the case."

"Maybe that's been done, but you haven't been told?"

"None of the lads has mentioned carrying out such inquiries . . . But what the hell. It's not my problem." He silently wished he could convince himself of that.

Sixteen

The rain had ceased, but the gloomy clouds which covered the sky promised a quick resumption. The CID Vauxhall from G Division led the Land Rover from Vehicles into Hamsworthy. "I lived the other side of this place when I was a kid," Detective Inspector Swift said.

"Yeah?" Detective Sergeant Chadwick didn't give a damn where the other had spent his childhood. As he braked to avoid a dog, he gloomily reflected on the burden of having to suffer a gabby senior officer. And not only gabby, but inconsistent. One minute friendly, the next pulling rank so hard that it was like being expected to stand to attention at the salute. In two months and six days, he was due to retire. Alleluia! And even if his replacement was a cold-eyed bastard on the promotion trail, at least one would always know where one stood . . .

"Of course, the town was much smaller then. Near our place was a small bakery which made the crispest cottage loaves. You don't see 'em now, do you?"

"Can't really say."

"In fact, you don't find any proper bread most of the time, just the wrapped stuff. Sliced pap, I call it."

They passed a row of houses built in the locally produced yellowish bricks which added a touch of premature decay.

"Doughnuts were a penny each. They filled them with raspberry jam from a paper cone . . . Although come to think of it, it can't have been paper because that would never have pierced the doughnut. Cardboard, I suppose. Only it was squeezable and it's difficult . . ."

Chadwick gloomily thought that it wouldn't be long before he was regaled with the DI's first baby words.

They approached lights. Swift said: "Turn left."

"According to Frank we should go right."

"Are you telling me that I don't know where Morton Manor is? We used to wonder how anyone could be rich enough to live in such a palace. It was the local MP owned it – a real Tory squire."

Chadwick moved the blinker column to show he would be turning left; the driver of the Land Rover sounded its horn three times in quick blips.

"What's up with him?" Swift asked.

"Like I said, Frank reckons we turn right."

"You can tell him from me he should always study the correct route before setting off."

The lights were in their favour and they turned left, entering a confusing maze of roads which ran through a large housing estate.

"This is all new," Swift complained. "I don't recognise anything."

"Maybe we should turn back and try the other road?"

"Carry on."

They carried on until Swift finally accepted the need to ask someone for directions. Rounding a corner, two women were approaching on the nearside pavement. Chadwick braked to a halt and stepped out on to the road to speak to them across the roof of the car. Their manner wary, because this was an area where caution was always advisable, they consulted each other and finally decided they didn't know where Morton Manor was. One road further on, a postman delivering mail was more helpful and able to give precise directions.

As Chadwick settled behind the wheel, he said: "It's

back to the lights and then take the road in the other direction."

Swift had nothing to say; and even less when they reached Morton Manor to find the Land Rover parked in front of the second and much smaller gateway in the eight foot high brick wall.

It was obvious that the large Georgian house had once stood proud of the town; now it was surrounded by modern semi-detacheds which had all the style of a limping hippopotamus.

"Tell them to wait here until we call them in," Swift said, as he opened the passenger door.

Chadwick left the car and walked the few feet to the Land Rover. "The Guv'nor says you're to hang on here until he shouts."

"To find out where he's got to?"

He joined Swift at the heavy metal gate by the side of which was an entryphone unit set in the brickwork. He pressed the call button. A voice made tinny by the speaker asked him who he was. "County CID."

The gate swung slowly open, to the accompaniment of metallic squeaks. They entered a very large garden with flower beds full of colour, manicured lawns, specimen trees, a fountain, and several pieces of statuary. As he followed Swift up the gravel path in which not a weed grew, Chadwick's thoughts were bitter – a not unusual occurrence. He was honest and so had to work his butt off just to keep a roof over his family's heads; Cairns thought honesty had died a long time before and could blow his nose on fifty-pound notes. If the world had been programmed, the programmer had a warped sense of humour.

They climbed three stone steps to an elegant portico. Chadwick rang the bell and the door was immediately opened by a thick-set man with a bruiser's face, dressed in good quality, casual clothes. He stared antagonistically at them.

"Is Mr Cairns in?" Swift asked.

"What if he is?"

"We'd like a word with him."

"What if he don't want to talk to the likes of you?"

"He'd be ill-advised." There was a snap to his words.

Swift could be more than a gabby middle-aged man, Chadwick thought reluctantly; when he tried, he became a reasonable imitation of a detective inspector.

"Wait."

They waited in the well-proportioned hall, on the walls of which hung several trophy heads.

A door at the far end opened and Cairns stepped into the hall. "Good morning, gentlemen. Would you care to come in here?" There was mockery in his politeness. He indicated the room he'd just left with a sweep of his right arm.

The large drawing room had decorative plasterwork and was furnished expensively and with considerable taste. Ronnie was seated in one of the luxurious armchairs.

"Ronnie, these two gentlemen are from the police."

"It would be a lie as well as a social solecism to say, 'Pleased to meet you,'" Ronnie lisped.

Cairns laughed. "Dear boy, our two visitors have the air of men at work, so perhaps it would be best if you left us."

"Are you sure you'll be safe?" he asked, using his pliant voice to give the word 'safe' a meaning he knew would infuriate the detectives. He stood and crossed to the doorway, with exaggerated movements, left.

"Do sit down, gentlemen. And let me offer you a drink before we get down to discussing whatever it is has brought you here."

"Nothing, thanks," Swift replied, showing no resentment

119

at Cairns's manner, which showed as much contempt as had Ronnie's.

"Then at least do sit."

They sat. "We're investigating a fatal car accident."

"A constant recurring tragedy, so painful for all concerned."

"It occurred on the twenty-second of last month."

"Where?"

"Near Clevestone, close to the south coast."

"That's a long way away. I wonder why you think it might concern me?"

"We've reason to believe your Mercedes was involved."

"An extraordinary idea!"

"An eyewitness to the fatal accident was able to note the registration number. That number identifies your car."

"Poor man! His eyesight must be very faulty. Isn't it extraordinary what mistakes people can make?"

"The accident occurred when a boy on a motor scooter lost control and came out of a farmyard directly in front of the path of the oncoming car."

"Then how can you blame the driver?"

"His offence was not to stop after the accident."

"That doesn't sound serious enough to bring someone as senior as you to my humble home."

"It's a crime and our job is to investigate all crime. The car hit the scooter and ran over the boy. As always, there'll have been a transfer of traces and if there is a suspect vehicle these can confirm or deny that that vehicle was involved. Since you assure us it was not your car which was involved, I take it you'll be willing for us to check it over and confirm the fact?"

"I'll give it to you straight. Being suspected gets me feeling bloody-minded – it would you, wouldn't it? But there's the other side of the coin. The law has to be supported, or where would we all be? So I'm saying I'm not happy you could possibly suspect me, but I am happy to do whatever I can to help."

"Then we may drive your Mercedes to our vehicle testing station for it to be examined?"

"Why not? I've a couple more cars if I need 'em."

Swift stood and Chadwick followed suit. Swift said: "May we have the keys?"

"They'll be in the car."

"Which is where?"

"The garage. But there's just one thing before you go. According to what I've heard, when you lot take something for checking, it can go missing . . ."

"That's balls!" Swift interjected with sudden, sharp anger.

"I wouldn't know. But being a cautious kind of man, very conservative with a small c, I think I'd like a receipt. You do give receipts, I suppose?"

Swift, outwardly calm, inwardly cursing, wrote out a receipt for one Mercedes SL 500.

They did not bother to say goodbye. As Chadwick opened the front door, Ronnie stepped into the hall from one of the rooms to their left.

"I do hope you've had a satisfying time," he lisped.

Chadwick slammed the front door behind himself. In the road, he spoke to the two in the Land Rover. "Here are the keys of the Merc. You'll find it in the garage."

"He's being a good boy, then, and cooperating?"

"Only because he knows the car's as clean as a virgin's diary," Chadwick said bitterly.

It was Vehicles' proud boast that if a car hit a fly they'd uncover traces of the impact.

They made a general inspection of the Mercedes, then concentrated on the front wings, especially the nearside one as this was presumed to have taken the force of the collision. They looked for signs of metal distortion which, however expert the repairer, could never be entirely avoided; for new paintwork; for anything that would indicate an entire new wing had been fitted; for underbody signs of damage contact. They checked the chassis and engine numbers to confirm that these matched the car to which the registration number had been issued. They found no sign of damage repair, no traces of impact, and all numbers matched.

Seventeen

On some days events flowed smoothly, on others they shattered against rocks. At six-thirty, Tuesday evening, Ballard was feeling exhausted, mentally more than physically, as he left the lift and made his way to the CID general room.

White looked up from his desk. "You're in great demand. The skipper's been shouting for you every quarter of an hour."

"The perils of popularity!" He sat, looked at his watch. Fleur and he were going to the cinema – that was, provided he didn't leave work too late . . .

Frost appeared in the doorway. "Where the hell have you been for the past several hours?" he demanded.

Ballard said: "I've been trying to find people who don't exist or have emigrated to Alaska; struggling to obtain statements from the deaf, the dumb, and the blind . . ."

"Get along to my room." He disappeared from sight.

"Was he born sour or did life sour him?" White asked thin air.

Ballard left and went along the short stretch of corridor to the detective sergeant's room. Frost was standing by his desk. "We've just received the report on Cairns's Mercedes." He went round the corner of his desk, sat. "It's clean."

"Impossible!"

"Try telling that to the blokes who examined it."

123

"Sarge, it was the car which hit the Kerr boy. It's got to be."

"What's it take to convince you of something? A brain transplant?"

"All the evidence says—"

"It says the car is clean so it can't have been involved in the accident. Which makes your theory yesterday's news."

"Then now what?"

"*Finito.*"

"But . . ."

"Can't you understand English?"

"*Bien entendu*! . . . Sarge, if I'm wrong, however many coincidences are we looking at? Enough to give a statistician nightmares. I have to be right and Cairns's Merc was taking the hit man down to the marina when it smashed into the scooter. But then it must have suffered damage which Vehicles would have uncovered. So if the car they examined is clean, it hasn't been in any accident."

"Which is what I've just said in a quarter of the words."

"Right. So it was a substitute. Knowing his car might be examined, Cairns—"

"How could he know?"

"He was warned by someone down here."

Frost said angrily: "Are you that sodding stupid you're trying to stitch up the DI again?"

"All I'm saying is that there is someone with access to information in this division who got word to Cairns. Cairns accepted that if his Mercedes was examined by Vehicles, they'd be able to determine beyond argument that it had been in the collision. So he moved really fast. Someone in his outfit nicked a green Mercedes CL five hundred of near enough the same age. Registration, engine, and chassis plates were switched.

"This wouldn't guarantee cover since plates can't be switched without leaving traces for a really sharp examiner to find. But Cairns could guess that attention would be fixed on the wing and underneath and when those were found to be clean, the examiners would conclude the car had not been involved in the accident; once that happened the intensity of their search would drop off. He was exactly right. The car's got to be examined again, this time specifically for changed plates."

"We ask Vehicles up North to waste even more time?"

"I'll stake my life it won't be wasted."

"The stake's not worth the risk."

"No? When there's a really good chance of landing Cairns at long last, identifying which copper is bent, and as a minor bonus, finally solving the hit-and-run case?"

After a moment, Frost said: "You can put it to the Guv'nor. I'm not going to make a fool of myself doing that."

Lock, seated, listened in silence, then turned to Frost, who stood by the side of Ballard. "What's your opinion?"

"I suppose it's possible, sir."

"But not probable?"

"Hard to judge."

"But that's what we have to do now."

There was a silence.

"There is a chance you could be right," Lock finally said, speaking to Ballard. "So I'll go ahead and make the request, hoping they don't get too steamed up because they think I'm questioning their efficiency."

The metal gate opened and Swift and Chadwick went through into the garden. One man, seated on a mower, was cutting the nearest lawn, another was weeding a flower bed. "Who said crime doesn't pay?" Chadwick asked bitterly.

The front door was opened by Ronnie. "Hullo, there," he

said, elongating the first word. "Lovely to meet you again. Would you like to follow me."

"Sooner than have you following us," Chadwick answered.

Ronnie giggled. "Naughty, naughty!"

Cairns was in a second and smaller sitting room whose most noticeable feature was the beautiful marble mantlepiece, the carving of which on close inspection proved to be of a very voluptuous nature.

"You'll have a drink this time?" Cairns asked.

"No," Swift replied shortly.

"What a very abstemious police force we have these days! Ronnie, dear boy, I'm sure it's again not a social visit so why not leave us and then you won't be upset if they start saying nasty things?"

"Perhaps I'll have a little sun by the pool."

"Don't forget, not too long. We don't want you to suffer from skin cancer."

"That's just too awful even to think about. I'll put lots and lots of blocking cream on." He carefully made his way out of the room.

"Such a charming young boy," Cairns said.

They kept their descriptions to themselves.

"Now, tell me what's the trouble this time?"

"We want to examine your Mercedes again," Swift said.

"Why?"

"There's something more we need to check."

"You still won't believe me when I say the car can't have been in the South on the day you talked about?"

"Have you any objection to us taking it away for a further examination?"

"I can only repeat what I said last time."

Swift stood.

"There is a problem now, though."

"What?"

"It's not mine any longer."

"How's that?"

"I've sold it. This may seem a little odd as it was hardly any age . . ."

"Bloody odd."

"Which is why I'll try and explain. You must understand I'm a man of great feeling; so great that I'm affected by matters which wouldn't disturb most people. After you returned the car, I was so distressed to think it had been a cause of unjust suspicion, I began to fear it was an omen of impending doom. I imagined being involved in some horrific accident. Ronnie understood exactly. I once bought him a beautiful gold chain and medallion, but it gave him bad vibes and he simply couldn't wear it. Such a shame since it suited him perfectly."

"Who did you sell it to?"

"I was simply delighted when he asked me if I'd mind giving it to a charity to help stray dogs and cats in Egypt. It's really distressing to think of so much misery . . ."

"The Mercedes."

"I thought of giving that to charity as well, but truth to tell, I'm afraid there has to be an end to one's generosity when one isn't rich."

"Did you sell it to the trade?"

Cairns massaged his plump jaw with forefinger and thumb. "I suppose you might call him that."

"Who's him?"

"A gentleman who claims to be Polish, but clearly is of very mixed origins. Ronnie suggested more than a touch of the Levant, but I think that's less likely than—"

"Where's his office?"

"A man of his ilk shuns fixed points of reference. Perhaps that is because he is forever travelling around this country, finding cars he likes, buying them and shipping them to

Poland where he sells them. At least, that is what he claims.
It is quite likely he sells them anywhere but in Poland. He
likes to play his life very close to his chest."

"His name?"

"I can't remember it and even if I could, I certainly
wouldn't be able to pronounce it. Polish is a language that
only a Pole can or should attempt to speak."

"How do you contact him?"

"Why should I? I am not in the car trade."

"Then how come you were able to sell him your car?"

"He phoned and asked me whether I would like to."

"Some coincidence that he should phone you after you'd
decided to get rid of it!"

"Coincidences abound. I only met Ronnie because we
both—"

"Why should he phone you?"

"An interesting question which, interestingly, I asked myself.
And I decided there can be only one answer. I must have mentioned I intended to sell to someone who was either in the trade
or talked to someone who was and that someone mentioned the
fact to him. Wouldn't you agree that that's what happened?"

"Nothing's less bloody likely," Chadwick said.

Cairns smiled.

The door was open so Ballard walked into Lock's room
without knocking. "You're shouting for me, sir?"

"I thought you should see this," Lock replied as he held
out a sheet of paper.

Ballard crossed to the desk to take the fax, read. "That's
one bummer of a story!"

Lock made no comment.

"He knew we were asking for a second examination of
the Merc, realised what this meant, got rid of it. This proves
I'm right."

"Hardly."

"But surely . . ."

"Using the word in its legal sense, the only way of proving you're right will be to examine the car's chassis and engine plates and find the evidence they have been exchanged."

"Then we find it."

"With nothing more to go on than Cairns's story, which will have as much relation to the truth as a politician's word of honour?"

"He'll have had it crunched. So we have all scrapyards questioned."

"To examine their records and question the staff would call for a coordinated operation from every force in the country. It takes the assassination of royalty or mugging of a pop star to bring that about."

"That man who called on Aldridge—"

"Spare me the repetition. What I'm saying basically is that although it may seem very likely Cairns has been fed information by the same person who set out to confuse Aldridge's evidence, we only have circumstantial evidence, which is weak, that such person actually exists. With so dubious a background, our only way forward is to hope that in time he will give himself away."

"You're closing the case?"

"In practical terms. That is, unless you can come up with another imaginative possibility. And if you do, try to remember I'd rather hear what it is from you directly than learn about it indirectly through your insubordination." Lock's tone remained pleasant even though it had sharpened.

"There has to be something we can do."

"A friendly word. Obsession and police work don't make good bedfellows."

*   *   *

"You're looking even tireder than usual," Winifred said as Ballard stepped into the hall of Ash Farm.

"Work has been heavy. Or seemed to be."

"That's an intriguing comment!"

Before he could answer the unasked question, Fleur came out of the sitting room. "I didn't hear the car arrive." She kissed him lightly on the cheek.

"He's exhausted," Winnifred said. "He needs some glucose."

Pearce appeared at the head of the stairs, having to hunch his shoulders slightly because of the sloping ceiling. "A stiff whisky would do the man a damn sight more good!" He descended the stairs. "Geoffrey, we'll go through and sort things out in a man's way."

"There isn't time for a drink," Fleur said.

"In a well-regulated home, there is always time."

"We're asked for eight thirty and I refuse to be late yet again." She turned to Ballard. "Ready?"

Ballard said goodbye to her parents and followed her out of the house and around to his car. As he settled behind the wheel, he said: "Your father's in good form this evening."

"He is, but as I keep telling you, he's not the stuffy person you seem to think."

He started the engine. "Not stuffy. Old fashioned."

"He'd take that as a compliment . . . Are you as tired as Mother obviously thinks?"

"I do feel a bit creased."

She put her arm along the back of his seat and rested her finger tips on his neck. "Too much work?"

"And frustration."

"So I'm partly to blame?"

He laughed. "For once, I wasn't meaning that kind of frustration."

"What kind, then?"

"People not believing me until too late."

"Is this still about the boy who was run over?"

He drove out of the yard and on to the road. "There's one last chance to prove I've been right from the beginning, but the DI's called a final halt to investigations."

"And you reckon he's wrong yet again?"

He drove around a sharp bend, at the apex of which was a very wide triangular verge in which grew a massive oak tree, before he answered her. "In theory, yes; in practice, no."

"It's a change to hear you even half agree with him."

"Maybe I've stopped being pig-headed."

"You said that, not I!" She brought her arm back and rested her hand on her lap. "So have you stopped suspecting him?"

"Yes."

"I'm glad. I rather like him and it would let the rest of you down so badly if he'd turned out to be crooked. Trust means so much in the force, doesn't it? Rather like marriage."

Eighteen

Ballard parked his car alongside Frost's and climbed out into the bright sunshine, which had returned over the weekend, and put the key under the front passenger seat. Later, Fleur's parents would drop her at the car park before driving up to Chelmsford to spend a couple of days with friends; Fleur would use his car to drive to Churley where a newly opened electrical store was holding a promotional sale. Some prices were advertised at a fifty per cent discount and she was hoping to be able to buy a food mixer and, perhaps, a microwave oven. Gradually, they were assembling all they would need to furnish their home. He walked towards the building. It appeared that the Mountforts were more and more inclined to refuse the tenant of their cottage a further lease and to sell. Life had golden edges.

Life changed colour at twelve fifty-two, after he'd returned from the scene of a minor break-in. As he crossed the general room to his desk, Dean said: "There've been two phone calls for you. Both from the Fleming Hospital."

"Have you any idea what they're about?"

"All the woman would say was you're to ring reception as soon as you can."

The phone was on the desk next to his. He picked it up and carried it across, taking care the long flex did not sweep the papers on the desk on to the floor. "Did they give their number?"

"No. And I'm afraid I forgot to ask them what it was."

Ballard went across to the table by the noticeboard, on which were a number of dog-eared reference books and two loose folders of standing orders, almost pristine. He flicked through the pages of the local telephone directory, found the number he wanted, returned to his seat and dialled.

"Fleming Hospital."

"This is Police Constable Ballard. There was a message for me to ring you."

"One moment."

A pause, some clicks, and another woman said: "Mr Ballard, I'm afraid I have some bad news for you. Miss Pearce has had a car accident."

Ice speared his mind. "Oh, my God! Is she badly hurt?"

"We can't be certain yet exactly what her injuries are because she has to undergo a further examination, but we can say her condition is not critical . . ."

"What sort of injuries? Where's she hurt? Is she conscious?"

The speaker, used to dealing with the effects of shocked emotions, patiently explained she could not tell him any more than she already had except to add that Fleur was conscious and had asked them to get in touch with him.

"I'll come right away."

"It may be a little time before you can see her because the doctors will have to complete their examination first."

He replaced the receiver without thanking her or saying goodbye.

"Who's in trouble?" Dean called out.

"Fleur's had an accident." He stood. "I've got to go and see her. They said she's not critical, but . . . but it sounds as if it could be bad."

"Not if she's not in a critical condition," Dean said, trying to offer some comfort even while acknowledging that his words were meaningless. They both knew that a man could be horribly beaten up, in agony, and facing a broken future, but in hospital language his condition was not critical.

"I'll tell the sarge . . ."

"I'll do that. You get off, and for God's sake drive carefully; don't try to get there before you've started. It doesn't need both of you as patients."

"She was in my car . . ."

"Then you want a taxi. I'll shout for one while you get below."

Fleming Hospital was on the outskirts of Staple Cross, and during the fifteen-minute drive Ballard's mind plumbed fear and despair.

On arrival, he rushed from the taxi towards the entrance and had to be recalled by a shout to pay the fare. The reception area was designed – so the 'Patients' Introduction To Us' claimed – to spread an air of calm; it failed completely to lessen the tension that gripped him until he seemed to have difficulty with breathing. His voice was croaky when he gave his name at the main desk and asked for news of Fleur. He was told to wait and it was suggested he sat.

He could not sit. He paced the floor, passing and repassing framed prints on the walls without once noticing their subjects. There was a middle-aged woman he did notice because she sat at the end of the row of seats which lined a wall and looked as if she was completely untroubled. Absurdly, he hated her for her mental peace.

A woman with a face made stern by its length asked him if he was Geoffrey Ballard.

"How's Fleur?"

"Just follow me, will you?"

He could have throttled her for not answering his question. Silence so often meant the worst . . .

She led the way into a small room with three chairs

set around a glass-topped table. "I've just finished my examination of Fleur. I'm happy to say she has not suffered the internal injuries we first feared."

It took time for the words to make sense. "She's not dying?"

"Far from it."

He sat. For an eternity – time had ceased to be measurable from the moment of the phone call – he had known such black fear that it was difficult to rid himself of it. He looked up. "That's the truth?"

She smiled, banishing the suggestion of severity. "Pure and unadulterated truth. Fleur has suffered a simple fracture, which has been set, and considerable bruising, but those are the extent of her injuries."

"Can I see her?"

"Yes. You may find her a little woozy from shock and the aftermath of the anaesthetic, but that's all."

He was directed to the fourth floor and room 311. He knocked, heard Fleur call out, went in.

The room had two beds; she lay in the right-hand one, the other was empty. There was sticking plaster on her right cheek, her left arm was in plaster from wrist to elbow; her hair was untidy and her lipstick smudged. For him, she had never looked more beautiful.

When he bent down and kissed her, he was trembling. Words choked him.

"What a to-do!"

It was what she often said when they brought their love-making to an end because if they did not it would not end until it ended.

"Darling, you must do something for me. Take my keys to the house, go up to my bedroom, open the bottom drawer of the chest-of-drawers and bring me a couple of my nightdresses. The one they've given me to wear must

135

have come from a Victorian charity ward. And also some toilet things so I can make myself look half normal."

"Will do."

He went to sit on the chair.

"Here."

She patted the bed.

He sat and she gripped his hand; for a while, words that were not spoken passed between them.

She broke the silence. "I'm terribly afraid your car's a write-off. I'm so sorry."

"Forget it."

"But I can't. It is comprehensively insured, isn't it? That means the insurance company should give you enough to buy another, shouldn't it?"

"Stop worrying about something that doesn't matter."

"I'll bet you don't think that when you're at home and wondering how to get to work."

"I'll catch a bus."

"Thinking, 'Another hopeless female driver?'"

"No. Just thank God it wasn't worse."

She raised his hand and kissed it, released it, adjusted the line of the sheet which came up just above her breasts, went to move her left arm and gasped.

"Is it hurting very badly?" he asked, mentally shrinking from the thought of the agony she must be suffering.

"Just a twinge. They've given me a painkiller and it's doing its job most of the time."

"Do you want something stronger? Shall I find a nurse and ask her to get you it?"

"There's no need. I promise you I'm all right. Poor darling! You're suffering more than I am."

"Hardly."

"Mother has said more than once that she's surprised

136

someone as emotional as you should join the police. Did you know that?"

"I didn't."

"She's become very fond of you, in part because she reckons you're so good for me." She smiled. "And I always agree with her! . . . When they were getting me out of the car, it was you in my mind, not them, yet I love them nearly as much . . . Isn't it funny how the mind works? When I saw I was going to hit the tree, I didn't think, "Help!", my life didn't race through my mind, I remembered that I hadn't returned the patterns the dressmaker lent me. What do you think a psychiatrist would make of that?"

"It's safer not to wonder. Are you up to telling me what happened?"

"Of course I am, since I wasn't doing anything silly. I was coming back from Churley . . . The food mixer! I've forgotten all about it. Still, the policeman was very charming and assured me everything would be safe, just before they put me into the ambulance. I didn't get a microwave because they only had a couple in the sale and I didn't recognise the brand. We can easily manage without one."

"You were driving back from Chorley and then what?"

"As I told the policeman who questioned me very briefly, I was going slowly – I couldn't make up my mind whether to turn off and have ten minutes with Anne who's only a couple of miles from the main road. Anyway, I went to brake for the sharp corner just past the farmers' stall that's there and the pedal went straight down to the floorboards. I tried to change into a lower gear and steer round, but the car skidded into a tree that's growing exactly in the right place to catch someone sliding off the road."

"You lost the brakes?"

"No. I knew where they were . . . Not very amusing?"

"I'm sorry, it's just that I'm in total mental turmoil."

"So am I. But I release pressure by being facetious. Very English, Father would say approvingly."

"Wasn't there any pressure left in the pedal?"

"There might have been a little, but I can't remember. Of course, if I'd been smart, I'd have managed to change up, but all I produced was a terrible noise."

"The car was serviced just over a fortnight ago. How could the brakes fail? If some mechanic forgot to check the brake fluid reserve, I'll murder the bastard!"

"Don't do that. Someone might find out and when I'm back on my feet I'd have to visit you in prison and I'd hate to do that."

"But you could—"

"Have been killed. I suppose I would have been if I hadn't been wondering about Anne. It's quite a thought, isn't it?"

She was trying to smile, but he could be certain that the thought of what might have been frightened her as much as it did him.

The garage was on the main road to the south of Staple Cross, near the railway station. A modern five-floor glass and brick building fronted workshops which dated back to the early fifties; on the left-hand side was a showroom in which one dazzlingly clean Peugeot and one mud-encrusted one with racing numbers and a multitude of commercial stickers were on display. He told the young woman behind the reception desk that he wanted to speak to the foreman; his manner caused her to call the manager.

"Hullo, Mr Ballard, good to see you again," said the manager as he entered through the doorway at the back of the reception area. Normally, he would not have been so welcoming to someone who was not a particularly profitable customer, but one never knew when it would pay to have the goodwill of a policeman. "How can I help you?"

"My fiancée was driving my car this morning and had a crash."

"I'm very sorry indeed to hear that. I do hope she wasn't injured?"

"She was. The brakes failed. But you serviced the car a fortnight ago."

The manager's expression became defensive.

"So what the hell kind of a service did you carry out?"

"A complete, thorough—"

"Crap!"

"Mr Ballard, I assure you—"

"She would have been killed if she hadn't been driving very slowly – because whoever did the work on my car was either incompetent or dead lazy."

"I'm sorry to hear you say that. We're proud of the high standard of our work and if you'll have the car brought here, I'll personally make certain that a thorough examination is carried out and the cause of the brake failure is found."

"And have you lot fob me off with some cock-and-bull story that leaves you in the clear?"

"Of course not."

"I'm going to have the police experts make the examination so that the truth comes out."

"There can be no question of negligence on our part. Our staff a—"

"Incapable of doing a proper job." Ballard turned and left. He accepted that he had mishandled the meeting, but had been unable to prevent his fear, which perversely had grown not diminished since the accident, provoking illogical anger.

The manager eased his way past a car on a hoist to the corner of the second workshop where two men in oil-stained overalls were bent over the engine of an ancient 309. "Fred."

Penrose, the older man, stepped back and straightened up.

139

"I need a word."

The manager returned to his office, sat behind the desk. When Penrose entered, he said: "D'you know Mr Ballard?"

"Can't say I do."

"He's a copper."

"There's more than one of 'em comes here."

"You're down on the computer as having serviced his car a fortnight ago tomorrow."

"Then I guess I serviced it. So?"

"You did check everything really thoroughly, especially the brake system, didn't you?"

"What sort of fool question is that?"

"His woman was out in the car this morning and the brakes failed. She got injured. He's just been here shouting his head off and accusing us of negligence. I offered to have the car checked to find the cause of the failure, but he's going to get his own outfit to do that because he doesn't believe we'd make an honest job of it . . . Now you think about things, maybe you can remember working on his car and doing a real thorough job?"

"Sure."

"Paying special attention, like always, to the braking system?"

"Right."

"That's what I told him. But he didn't seem to want to believe me."

Nineteen

Ballard spoke to the insurance company's representative over the phone. Yes, she said, in a voice which suggested crooked little fingers and cucumber sandwiches, the claim would naturally be settled as quickly as possible – but he must understand that certain details had to be ascertained and certain procedures carried out before actual payment was made. And no, compensation would not be for the amount insured, but for the street value of the vehicle.

As he replaced the receiver, he composed a new motto for the insurance business. Take owt, pay nowt.

Turner lent him an ancient Vespa and he used this to go between the flat, divisional HQ, and the hospital. On Friday evening, Fleur greeted him with the news: "They're letting me out tomorrow morning after the doctor's made one last check that I'm all in one piece. Probably it'll be around eleven."

He kissed her a second time to celebrate.

"Mother wants to know if they should pick you up on their way in to collect me."

"I'm sorry, darling, but I'm not going to be able to get away until the evening."

"Can't you ask for a little time off for the special circumstances? Or aren't I special circumstances?"

"More special than special. But the answer would be no even if I got down on hands and knees; we're short-handed again."

141

"Still, you'll be along later?"

"As fast as the scooter will get me to you."

"It'll take for ever. I'll get Father to collect you."

"Don't bother the old boy. If he collects me, he has to run me back and he says he doesn't like driving at night."

"Because he feels he can't have more than one glass of wine with the meal."

"You're very unkind!"

She laughed.

"I'll be fine. The Vespa doesn't burn rubber, but it's surprising how quickly it gets one to anywhere."

"Are you sure?"

"Couldn't be more certain."

"But—"

"It's settled."

"The masterful male? Have you remembered to use that masterfulness to tell the insurance company to provide you with a car until they pay up?"

"They referred me to my policy and this article and that clause and this sub-clause which excludes any such thing."

"That makes me feel even more guilty."

"Don't be ridiculous."

"But I was driving."

"It wouldn't have mattered if Schumacher had been at the wheel; no brakes, no stop."

"But he'd have managed to get a lower gear, or spin the car, or something. I was talking to Mother about you having to go everywhere on the scooter and how worried I was because they're so dangerous and if it rains you get wet."

"What's a little double pneumonia in the pursuit of love?"

"Shut up! . . . Mother made a suggestion. They're giving us that ten thousand as a wedding present and Father's been trying to find out legally how to avoid the tax on the gift; Mother's not quite so transparently honest when it comes to taxation and she says why don't they lend you the money for another car? Then, when the insurance people pay up, you can bank it in your name and forget to pay back what you've borrowed . . . She says Father's worried because maybe it's not quite pukka and you're a policeman so you've got to be whiter than white, but she'll persuade him that it would be very sensible and quite OK."

The door opened and an elderly woman, wearing an old-fashioned woollen dressing gown, stepped inside, then came to a halt. "I didn't know you'd someone here, love. I'll go back and watch the telly a bit more."

"It's quite all right . . ." She stopped as the other left and closed the door. "They put her in here yesterday. Quite a dear, but does she snore! Do you snore?"

"I've no idea. Share my bed and find out."

"We'll leave that until we're married just in case you do; then it'll be too late for me to cry off."

Vehicles at county HQ rang on Monday, a week after the crash. "One of the brake lines ruptured, as a consequence of which there was loss of fluid, unequal braking and then a very rapid lack of all braking power."

"Could that be due to incompetent servicing?" Ballard asked.

"No."

"Then what?"

"Not easy to say."

"Come on, Sarge, you're the expert."

"Metal can simply fracture because of a flaw, undetectable in the normal course of events, that is aggravated by vibration or some other cause of fatigue: or it can do so because it's weakened by a blow. That's what most likely happened here."

"The car ran over something that was thrown up?"

"It's difficult to work out exactly how that could happen, seeing where the fracture occurred. More likely there was a direct blow."

"A spanner slipped during the servicing?"

"That's possible."

"You could sound vaguer if you really tried."

"The thing is . . . Look, do you know anyone who could want you to have an accident?"

The question was so unexpected, it took a couple of seconds for him to appreciate its import. "You're saying this was sabotage?"

"It's possible the line was deliberately damaged, but if it was, it was done so skilfully that we can't be certain."

He stared at the desk, not seeing it, but Fleur in a car that must crash.

"Are you still there?"

"Yes," he answered hoarsely.

"So it really comes down to the question of whether it's likely there is someone who could want to harm you. If there is, the marks could mean a lot, if there isn't, they're not of any direct consequence and the crash was one of those very unfortunate accidents. Bloody bad luck for your girlfriend, of course, but that's it. OK? The next time you're around this way, you can show your gratitude with a couple of pints."

He managed a few words of thanks, rang off.

White, the only other person in the room, stood. "If the sarge starts yelling for me, tell him I'm beavering on the Allen case. I've a snout who says he's some interesting information, only I can't yet make out if he's more full of wind than facts." He left.

Ballard stared into space. If there was no one who wished him ill, the crash had been an accident; if there were someone who might, it could have been a deliberate attempt on his life. If. Goddamn it, life was full of ifs and now so was death. If Cairns had had to scrap his new Mercedes and replace it because his part in the murder of Jenner was in danger of being exposed, he would have cause enough to hate the man who had placed him in that peril. He could only have known the identity of the man if there were a traitor amongst the police . . . If he had been driving the car, his rhythm of braking would have been different from Fleur's and he would probably have been going more quickly – certainly so at the moment of fracture – and could so easily have died. The failure to kill him would become known and there might well be a second attempt. If there were, it would probably be more direct – a petrol bomb into the newsagent under his flat in the middle of the night, a plastic explosive bomb fixed to his next car so that Fleur might again be a victim as well as he. What if she were fatally injured, but he survived to have to live with the tragedy?

However rollercoaster had been his previous suspicions, logic now said loudly and clearly that if there were a traitor, he could only be the detective inspector. Because Fleur's life was at stake, he had to try and confirm or deny the possibility, no matter at what cost to himself.

It was easier to make a decision than to decide how to implement it. But there was one step he could take, even if it had not been done before because the chances of success had appeared too slight to be worth the effort.

Mrs Aldridge opened the front door of the cottage. "You want my husband? He's out at the back, gardening."

"Is it all right if I go round and have a word with him?"

"That path'll take you." She pointed. "And when you've done, you'll maybe like a cup of tea?"

"Thanks, but I am a bit rushed for time."

In the kitchen garden were rows of peas, beans, tomatoes, cabbages, potatoes, other vegetables he could not identify, in different stages of growth. Aldridge was on his knees in the small greenhouse, firming down some transplanted lettuces.

"Morning," Ballard said. It was obvious from the way

Aldridge looked at him that he had not been immediately recognised. A poor omen. "Detective Constable Ballard, local CID. I've been here before."

Aldridge straightened up and then pressed his hands into the small of his back to ease aching muscles. He moved his jaws as if chewing something.

"Do you remember telling me how on the evening of the accident a policeman called here when your wife was out and he asked questions and the way he went on and on about the difficulty of you correctly reading the car's registration number which got you a little confused?"

"Aye," Aldridge answered, but didn't sound very certain.

"Would you recognise the man who came here if you saw a photo of him?"

There was a long pause. "I suppose I might."

"Have a look at this." Ballard held out a large photograph which had been taken at the last annual divisional dance, a tradition that almost all would have liked abolished, but had not been because no one had the neck to challenge the belief that it was good for morale; it featured several members of CID and four guests. Is he in this group?"

Aldridge took the photograph in hands lightly crumbed with earth and stared at it. "I need me reading glasses," he said. "Can't read things without 'em."

Ballard, suffering the tension of hope, however unrealistic, said sharply: "Where are they?"

"Indoors."

"Then let's go back to the house."

They left the greenhouse and went up the grass path to the house. In the kitchen, Aldridge shouted: "Where are me glasses?"

"Wherever you left 'em," his wife called back from beyond the kitchen.

"She hides 'em," Aldridge muttered. "Deliberate."

Ada entered, a case in her hands. "Like I keep telling you, you need to hang 'em around your neck."

He took the case from her, opened it, put on the glasses, studied the photograph. "I can't see nothing. These are me telly glasses."

"Then you put 'em in the wrong case. If I weren't around to find you, you'd lose yourself." She turned and left the room.

"Don't never know what she's doing or saying," he mumbled with deep, unjustified and ungracious satisfaction.

She returned, brought a second pair of glasses out of a case. "Here you are. Now give me the ones you've got and I'll put 'em in this. It's brown for reading, green for the telly."

"There ain't no call to go on and on telling me what I know." He put on the second pair of glasses, looked at the photograph again.

"Do you recognise anyone there?" Ballard asked.

Aldridge gave no answer, brought the photograph closer.

"He don't never remember faces," Ada said.

"Well, this time I bloody well do!"

"You recognise the man who came here that evening and said he was a detective?" Ballard asked, his voice reflecting his sharp excitement.

"I ain't so stupid as what she's always saying."

He moved until he could look at the photograph. "Which was the man who came here?"

A thick thumb, with dirt-filled nail, pointed to a guest, a man of fifty who owned a small chain of garages.

Ballard, his disappointment razor sharp, could cheerfully have told Aldridge a few home truths.

Twenty

D oe was left to carry his cases up to his room because he had the look of a man who thought 25p a generous tip. He closed and locked the door, placed one case on the bed, undid the straps, opened the lid and stared down at the Holland and Holland .450 Express, ran the tips of his fingers along the barrels and mentally compared their icy smoothness with the warm smoothness of a woman's inner thighs.

He closed the case and secured the two straps, crossed to the window and stared out at the street. Traffic was heavy and the pavements were crowded. He saw a middle-aged man, dressed with unusual formality in a pin-striped suit, and aligned imaginary cross-wires on his forehead . . .

It was going to be difficult. Hastings had made no secret of that fact. The problem wouldn't be the actual killing, it would be the lack of support, both to set up the job and to make an escape afterwards. He was entirely on his own because that was what the job demanded.

Uncertainty was the seed bed for nightmares. Had the car been sabotaged? Because he had not been killed, would a second attempt be made? Was Fleur in danger of becoming an active target rather than one by mistake, because failure had shown the would-be assassin that her death could cause him more pain than anything else?

To perceive the danger was, in his present state, to accept its certainty. He became convinced that her only chance of safety lay in their not being together and for two days he did not see her, pleading the intensity of work . . .

It was obvious that his state of fear and tension could not continue indefinitely or he would suffer a mental storm – he had to find a way of uncovering the truth. Yet every past attempt to do so had failed. Because a traitor had made certain it would? That was part of the still hidden truth. Was there a lead he'd missed? The yacht! If she had sailed from Gransere with Jenner's assassin aboard, it seemed probable the owner was directly connected with the assassination. A fact which on its own was meaningless. But mention of Spain had occurred before. Hastings, believed to be still in strategic command of the mob while Cairns was in tactical control, was rumoured to be living in Spain, known for its relaxed attitude towards the extradition of those who were wealthy and living within its boundaries. Find Hastings. How? Assume the yacht was owned by him and find the yacht, so find him. But this was to complete the circle of the unknown . . .

Perhaps the lead was bound to fail through lack of facts, yet it could still be useful. Suggest to Lock it should be followed up. If Lock agreed, he didn't fear the consequences of success and therefore couldn't be a traitor. Cairns had not been told by him the identity of the man responsible for placing him in danger of arrest, and therefore no act of revenge – the crash had been an accident. Fleur would be safe. The nightmare would be over . . .

He hurried along to Lock's room, to find it empty. He checked the time and was surprised to find it was after eight o'clock. The DI must have left for home some time before. Common sense said to wait until the morning to speak to him, but his fears for Fleur's safety, his certainty that he had discovered a way of finding out whether those fears were justified, overruled common sense. He'd beard Lock at home.

Back in the general room, he phoned Ash Farm. Winifred answered, called Fleur. Fleur said: "You promised to be here by seven and it's already eight."

"I know, darling, but work's piled up and up. How's the arm?"

"All right. Are you coming straight over?"

"I can't."

"It'll be dinner in half an hour."

Dinner was always at half-past eight; her father liked a regulated life. "I'm afraid you'll have to leave me out. Apologise to your mother and say how sorry I am."

"What's going on?"

"It's just that there's so much work . . ."

"We haven't seen each other for two days."

"Don't I know that!"

"Is something wrong?"

"Nothing. And when things ease off, I'll take you to Bora Bora and we'll lie on the hot, golden sand under a coconut tree."

There was a brief pause, then she said: "I'm not going to do that. Coconuts probably fall when they're ripe and I don't want to be crowned."

Her answer assured him she was reconciled to his further absence. He said he loved her so much he felt as if he were walking on helium, was unsurprised when her only response was "Me too"; in an old house, sound travelled and her parents were probably within earshot.

Please God, he thought, that the detective inspector agree immediately to pursue the lead.

Doe had bought a BMW bike because in the coming days reliability would be more important than sheer speed. He equipped himself with full leathers and a helmet with a dark, reflective visor; as effective as any mask, yet guaranteed to be unremarked.

He was a keen, skilled motorcyclist and enjoyed the hour-long ride; when he had enough money in the various accounts – never put all your eggs in one basket had been one of his mother's favourite sayings; she had seldom had any eggs to put anywhere – he would retire and live a life of sybaritic pleasures.

He had memorised the route from a map and followed this without a single wrong turn – he was very proud of a near photographic memory. Fifteen minutes later, he left the town, his thoughts more focused. It was going to be tricky, as Hastings had suggested. There was no empty office conveniently placed, as there had been before; just occupied houses. Without any back-up, no diversion could be created, no help given if something went wrong. But in a perverse manner, he was pleased that it was like this. There would be more satisfaction from doing the job well.

An open Aston Martin overtook him and the passenger was strikingly beautiful in a cool, bored manner; the kind of spoiled female who expected the best and was never satisfied when offered it. She reminded him that he must arrange a woman; a woman more easily contented.

Ballard had bought a second-hand red Peugeot 205 which, he had been assured, had been cosseted by its only proverbial elderly owner; to judge by the unblemished paintwork and the smoothness with which it ran, the salesman might for once have been speaking the truth.

He turned into Ekstone Road and found a parking space immediately in front of the Locks' house. As he switched off the engine and unclipped the seat belt, he hoped with an intensity of feeling that Lock would agree to trying to trace Hastings through the yacht, thereby bringing an end to suspicion and fear.

He left the car, crossed the pavement, opened the wrought-iron gate, walked up the short path to the front door, rang the bell. The door was opened by Karen. "This is a very unexpected pleasure!" she said and smiled.

He found himself wondering if this greeting, backed by a smile that might suggest more than facetious amusement, held unspoken offers. Angrily, he asked himself how, with six words, could she divert him from a matter which might well concern life or death? Did he have the mind of a sex-starved jellyfish?

"A case of no comment! Then perhaps we should become more formal. Good evening, how can I help you?"

"Is the inspector here, Mrs Lock?"

"What a short memory. The last time you were here, I asked you to call me Karen. Is it a name you have reason to dislike?"

"No."

"Then it was just forgetfulness? When there's cause, I always remember names. Yours is Geoffrey. I don't know why, but it always makes me think of knights in shining armour. I don't suppose you think of it in that light since every policeman I know seems to think chivalry has something to do with knives. Do come through."

He followed her into the sitting room, expecting to meet Lock; the room was empty.

"Why not sit down?"

He sat. She settled opposite him on the settee and since her skirt was as short as on his previous visit, he was again offered a view of much of her thighs. He had not deliberately looked, but he had seen; he jerked his gaze away. "The inspector is here, isn't he?"

"Is that a serious question?"

"Yes, of course."

"How disappointing!"

"Perhaps you'd tell me – I am in a bit of a hurry."

"Men are always in such a rush."

A meaningless comment to which he found himself adding meaning. Was she Circe, turning him into a swine with her magical arts?

"You seem to be a man of very few words, Geoffrey. Clearly, the strong, silent type."

"I've a lot on my mind."

"All very interesting, no doubt?"

Her tone had been one of knowing satisfaction. He corrected his thoughts. She'd merely spoken another meaningless comment to try to ease along a conversation that was proving difficult because he was making a complete berk of himself.

"I think a drink is called for. What would you like?" She stood with one easy, fluid movement.

"Nothing, thanks."

"I'm beginning to think that's your sole reply."

"Is the inspector here?"

"I am alone. And as I mentioned last time, absurdly I have a reluctance to drink when I am. Which is why I'm offering you the chance of giving me pleasure."

Yet again, he found himself adding a meaning to the words which, he then assured himself, was not intended.

"Your order, kind sir?"

He was sure he should refuse a second time, leave; then if in truth temptation had beckoned, he would have blocked his ears with wax to escape the siren's enchanting song . . .

"Gin, whisky, brandy, my favourite Rossi, or sweet vermouth?"

Someone else took possession of his tongue. "I haven't had Rossi in a month of Sundays," he heard himself saying.

"Enjoyment relived is enjoyment doubled."

He promised himself that this time he wouldn't watch her cross to the door, but he did. The tight-fitting dress moved lubriciously up and down her buttocks . . . As she left the room, he addressed himself. You've been suffering from great

153

mental strain and your mind is, without your will, harping on other things as a way of relieving that stress. You do not in truth lust after the detective inspector's wife; you are engaged to Fleur and love her far, far too much to foul that love by wandering into other fields . . . Some women were born teasers, advertising their availability until this was claimed, then gaining pleasure from denial. Karen was a teaser. Were he to make an advance, she would scornfully and indignantly deny she had given the slightest encouragement for such crude, ignorant, insulting behaviour. 'Many a dangerous temptation comes to us in gay, fine colours.' 'I can resist everything but temptation.' 'Saints resist temptations, wise men enjoy them.' Forget those last two . . .

She returned with glasses in her hands.

"When's the inspector returning?" he asked.

She came to a halt immediately in front of him. "You really don't know? And here have I been presuming you were certain he won't be back from the symposium for senior officers until tomorrow evening and your stated desire to speak with him was mere delicacy."

This was the end to double meanings. He had to leave . . .

"Your drink, sir." She leaned forward to hand him the glass.

Gravity altered the shape of her breasts and the low cut V-neck of her frock ballooned. As she began to lean, he promised himself not to look. He looked. She was not wearing a brassière and the smooth flesh was visible almost down to the nipples.

"I trust everything is to your satisfaction?" she said, as she straightened up. She returned to the settee and settled, her legs tucked under her, her frock now higher up her thighs. "What are you thinking, Geoffrey?"

"Nothing," he mumbled.

"I've always understood it's impossible to think of nothing because if you do, you're thinking of something . . . Would you draw the curtains for me? It's getting dark and I have an objection to the passers-by seeing what goes on."

He stood and crossed to the bay window, drew the two curtains. He started to return to the armchair.

"Wouldn't it be nicer to be more companionable? Pick up your glass and come and sit next to me." She patted the settee cushion to her side.

He swore to himself he'd return to the chair; he picked up the glass and went over to the settee, sat.

"Do you realise that you're a very interesting man?"

"Am I?"

"Most people, I can place; the Sam Turners of the world couldn't be more obvious. But you're different. How does one describe you? Thoughtful, intelligent, complicated? What would you say?"

"Very ordinary."

"I should, of course, have added too modest. Or is your modesty of the hypocritical persuasion? . . . I don't think so." She drained her glass. "Do we allow ourselves a second drink, remembering that wine is a turncoat, first a friend, then an enemy? Do you know who wrote that?"

"No."

"Nor do I. Didn't Shakespeare note the perils of drinking too much alcohol?"

"Yes."

"Do you think Sam even knows who Shakespeare is?"

"I expect so."

"You're a generous person, aren't you? But at least he'll be fully conversant with the more frustrating consequences of drinking too much . . . To risk is to live. Empty your glass and give it to me."

He drank what remained in his glass, handed it to her. She moved her legs, put her right hand on his shoulder to help herself rise up and stand; her fingertips brushed his neck and he seemed to feel electricity prickle his skin. He watched her walk out of the room and made no attempt not to visualise the flesh beneath the frock.

She returned, handed him one glass, settled on the settee with her legs under her. "What do we drink to?"

He shrugged his shoulders.

"That all our dreams come true?"

"Too destructive."

"Why?"

"If they're all fulfilled, what's left to yearn for?"

She laughed. "How typical! How very different! Sam would have rushed to drink to all his desires . . . But you never leap. You've learned the true secret of pleasure – delay." She drained her glass, put it down. "But there comes a time when further hesitation is impossible . . ."

She was staring directly at him and disturbingly he caught an expression of hatred in her strained expression and he thought she was about to prove herself to be the tease he had posited earlier. But then she reached for his hand and guided it high up her thighs.

Twenty-One

D oe was no skilled draughtsman, but if the sketch lacked finesse it contained all the details he needed to judge distances and angles, approach and escape routes. He sighed. His rifle would not be the best weapon of assassination, not least because it could quickly become a hindering bulk if events turned sour and he had to move quickly. It had helped him carry out many successful jobs and had become a talisman of success; he was loath to leave a talisman behind. But a realist faced facts. And being equally expert with a handgun, knowing a great deal about explosives, there were viable alternatives.

The high brick wall that encircled the house was a considerable obstacle, even though it could easily be scaled, because the only length not under direct observation from the road was on the south side where it formed the dividing wall between the very large garden of Morton Manor and the very small garden of the first of the comparatively mean houses. To climb the wall in sight of the road would be folly, so this had to be done along the stretch which divided the two gardens. There was no way of being sure who lived in the small house other than by spending a great deal of time watching it; time was short and he had no back-up. In the circumstances, he had to assume worst scenario – a large family. Then surprise and expert brutality very quickly delivered would be needed.

There was probably – perhaps better to say, certainly –

a security system covering the grounds of the manor; pressure and contact alarms, audible sensors, image-intensifying cameras linked to a computer system that would pick out movement. Without knowing for certain what system there was, which meant he couldn't previously judge best how to immobilise it, he would have to rely on speed; every security system ultimately depended on human reactions to its warning and reactions became sloppy as time went by if there were several false alarms and no genuine one.

Escape would have to be via his entry route. So if things did not go exactly according to plan and he was hotly pursued, the task of climbing the wall would be very dangerous. He would have to have some form of ladder which could be fixed to the inside of the wall before he approached the house . . .

He left the chair and crossed to the second suitcase, from which he brought a stolen mobile phone which had an altered chip that would record the call on some unsuspecting person's account. He punched in a number. When the connection was made, he said: "Abel?"

"Who's speaking?"

"Cain." He smiled. He had chosen the names for this childish rigmarole. "I want some goods."

"Such as?"

"A can of CS gas and two Mills bombs."

"Starting a war?" the speaker asked, his voice sharp with surprise.

He ignored the question. "Short-fused bombs."

"I can manage the can of gas. Don't know about the bombs."

"I was told you were the best. You'll find 'em."

"They'll cost."

"Name it."

"One K each?"

"With their detonators?"

158

"They wouldn't be much sodding use without, would they?" There was brief, sarcastic laughter.

"No," Doe agreed steadily. "But you could think you were being smart by trying to heist another thousand each before handing 'em over with fuses and then I'd have the trouble of teaching you it pays to be honest."

"Are you trying to threaten?"

"Explaining."

"Suppose I tell you where to put the bombs with the pins out?"

"You'd lose a good trade."

There was a pause. "It'll take time."

"Tomorrow."

"What's the panic?"

"That's my problem, not yours. I'll be in touch this evening to arrange delivery." He cut the connection. He often surprised himself by the curt authority he could summon when running a job. In normal times, he'd suffer a poor meal in a restaurant rather than register a complaint.

As Ballard lay next to Karen and stared up at the ceiling on which were patterns of light and shade from the elaborate bedside lights, he knew such contradictory emotions that it was as if his mind had suffered a fracture. He was bitterly ashamed that he had succumbed to temptation, proud of having aroused that temptation; he hated himself for having betrayed his love for Fleur, reassured himself that a casual one-night stand betrayed nothing since a man could always separate screwing from love . . .

Karen turned over and began to run her lips down his chest.

The phone rang.

She ignored it for a while, but finally raised her head. "That'll be Keith, wanting to make certain I'm safely tucked up in bed. I'll explain I'm too hot to have the bedclothes over me." She laughed as she clambered over him to pick up the phone which was on the table on his side of the bed; she made certain that his appreciation of her attractions was an intimate one.

That it was probably her husband phoning cleared his mind of any pride, left him contemptuous of himself; as a consequence, her wanton posture offended rather than inflamed. He tried to move, but she used her legs to prevent this.

"Hullo, darling . . ." She laughed. "I thought you were my husband . . . He's not here but at some sort of meeting and he won't be back before eight tomorrow evening . . . I'll tell him you called . . . Yes, we're having quite good weather . . . It's not that hot here . . . Goodbye." She replaced the receiver. "Wanted to waste time talking about the weather. Who the hell cares if it's ninety in Majorda, or wherever it is he lives? I should have told him that here it's been boiling!" She moved back until she could lie on top of him. After a while, she said: "What's the matter? The telephone call's delayed things and made the night go a little slack?"

The call had brought him to his senses. To try to assure himself that he had not betrayed his love for Fleur was the act of a coward; to have committed adultery (or was it just she who'd done that and he was guilty of fornication?) however great the temptation, was an act of cruelty aimed at the husband . . .

Once again, he tried to move free of her; this time, her action was more direct and soon his moral scruples weren't even a memory.

Back in his flat, Ballard suffered the torment of a conscience that was running at full revs. He'd always held in contempt those men who ignored their marriage vows, played the field, and laughed at women's tears. He stared down through the window at the pedestrians and motorists on their way to work. How many of them were also total hypocrites? How could he have trampled into the mud his love for Fleur by screwing

Karen, who at one point had almost seemed to be gaining more pleasure from the thought of betraying her husband than the actual act of betrayal?

All he wanted to do was forget the night, so it filled his mind. Would that he could scourge himself until the memories had to flee . . . Abruptly, he realised that there was one memory which was now haunting him and it was not that of tangled limbs. The phone call. Why should that hold significance other than to remind him of her husband because initially she had thought the caller to be he? The call had been from someone she patently didn't particularly like who apparently lived somewhere where the night temperature was over ninety. Then he certainly did not live in Britain. Karen had mentioned Majorda. The name meant nothing directly to him, yet irritatingly it seemed to echo somewhere he had heard about in Spain . . . Spain! Ballard's mind raced. Could Hastings have been phoning Lock? Because he had been screwing Karen, had he finally learned that Lock was a traitor? Could there then be a more bitter irony? . . . Or was he imagining an innocent call from friends to be a marker of betrayal because he was desperate to find something – however irrational – to lessen his sense of guilt?

The phone rang, startling him. He crossed the room, lifted the receiver.

"It's Winifred, Geoffrey."

He was sufficiently unnerved to suffer the absurd fear that Fleur's mother had learned about the previous night. "Good morning." His voice was croaky.

"Fleur was very worried because she phoned several times yesterday evening, but couldn't get an answer. She had to go to work early this morning, so asked me to get in touch and find out if you're all right. You don't sound too bright."

"I've started a cold." That explained his croaky voice, but not his silence. "I wasn't here last night because I was on a surveillance job." It was virtually certain the Pearces would

161

have received at least one phone call during the evening, so he added: "I only had one chance to speak to Fleur, but when I tried, your line was engaged."

"That was probably Elsie. She's such a chatterbox that one has to call on all of one's patience to remain interested in what she's talking about. Ian says that if he had to pay her phone bill, we'd be bankrupt . . . Are you sure you're only suffering from a cold?"

"That's all as far as I can tell." Add in an agonising conscience.

"Will you be along this evening?"

"I'm terribly sorry, but I can't say. The surveillance will probably continue."

"Surely they won't make you carry on if you have a nasty cold?"

"They'd jeer if I complained."

"Very Spartan! When Ian has a cold, he retires to bed and demands constant and personal attention."

He managed a brief laugh.

"If you can't get to us and have the chance, give Fleur a ring this evening."

"Of course."

"We look forward to seeing you almost as much as she does."

He said goodbye, replaced the receiver. She would have thought she was cheering him up with her final words, but she'd made his mood a shade darker. Betrayal caused so many ripples . . .

Did he have a chance to escape at least some of the ripples? Could the call have come from Hastings? The obvious way of finding that out was to ask Karen . . .

The nearer he approached Ekstone Road, the less optimistic he became. What in his flat had seemed to be a simple task gradually became one of daunting difficulty. His return so soon must surely make Karen believe it was eagerness to continue the liaison which brought him back, yet he was determined that whatever her guiles, there should be no continuation. How was he going to gain her cooperation without raising her anger when she understood he did not want to bed her again? Would she see his refusal as an insult? Somehow, he had to find a way of avoiding her frustrated fury, but how?

He turned into Ekstone Road. Perhaps he should start by telling her how magical the night had been. Women thrived on compliments. Then he could go on to explain that in view of their relationships with others, perhaps they should sacrifice themselves . . . Goddamn it, he thought, as he braked to a stop, even to himself, he was sounding like a pedantic, pompous loon. He switched off the engine. How about a *mea culpa*? Explain that he was so worried that his unforgivable, inexcusable behaviour must have caused her untold mental pain. But then it had been she who had made all the running.

He left the car, walked around the bonnet and on to the pavement. Whatever he said, he must avoid her gaining the slightest suspicion that what he sought was proof that her husband was a traitor . . .

He opened the gate and went up to the front door, rang the bell. As he waited, unwelcome memories of ever-mounting passion flooded his brain. What if she told him she would only answer his questions if he replayed that passion?

"Who is it?" she called out from inside.

"Geoffrey."

"Go away."

"All I want is . . ."

"For God's sake, go away and leave me . . ." Her words died away in sobbing.

He stood there. She had drawn him into her bed; when they'd parted, it had been only after she had demanded renewed passion. Yet now she rejected him amidst tears. He turned and began to walk slowly to the car. 'An' learn about women from me!' Was there a man fool enough to boast he understood the first thing about women?

Back in his flat, he overcame his bewildered disappointment sufficiently to work out that there was one other way in which he might be able to trace where the phone call had come from. He phoned the assistant librarian in the local public library, whom he knew casually. After the usual pleasantries, he asked her if she know where Majorda was. She asked him to spell the name and he gave her a phonetic rendering of what he remembered Karen's having said.

"Have you any idea where this place might be?"

"It could be Spain."

"Hang on and I'll see what I can find out."

A few minutes later, she came back on line. "I can't find a Majorda in Spain."

"Maybe I haven't got the name quite right. Is there somewhere that sounds very much like that?"

"I was going to say, there's Port de Majerda. That's on the Mediterranean coast, not far from the French border. Bert and I visited it a couple of years ago when we were having a fortnight's holiday in Lloret de Mar – we went there because he's mad keen on yachting. He had thoughts of buying a house on one of the canals until he found out how much that would cost."

"Are there big yachts there?"

"I suppose that depends on what you mean by 'big'. Certainly some of the ones we saw looked big to me. Of course, those can't go up all the canals, but there are two, or maybe it's three, which are deeper than the side ones and then there are berthing areas for the really large stuff. In some ways I'm glad we've no money – Bert's idea of a good time is to be wet through in the middle of a howling gale with sails torn to shreds, the emergency radio kaput, and seas crashing down on the fo'c'sle."

"Even the thought makes me feel queasy."

"I said to him, if ever we win the Lottery and you buy a boat and cross the Atlantic, like you're always saying you want to do, you'll go without me. And I added that if he needed a crew, I'd make certain they were all male. Not that that's such a good idea these days! . . . Sorry I can't do any more for you."

"You've been a tremendous help."

When the call was over, he returned to the window. There could come a point when there were too many coincidences even for the most careful man. Hastings was the power behind Cairns and as far as was known, he lived in Spain; the yacht in Gransere had been flying a Spanish flag; the phone call for Lock had been from someone who lived in a place whose name might be Majerda, which was a Spanish yachting centre . . .

It seemed he might have been given a final chance to discover if Lock, supposedly a role model, was in truth a traitor, and to make certain Fleur was safe. And there was a further prize to be gained. Prove Lock was a traitor and justification *could* be found – with a little help from hypocrisy – for having bedded Karen. After all, the modern world lived by the maxim that results always justified the means . . .

He checked his passport was in date; he phoned a local travel agent and asked which was the nearest commercial airport to Port de Majerda and when told Girona, said to book him a flight there as soon as possible. He phoned divisional HQ and spoke to Turner. "Sam, do me a favour. Tell the skipper I've gone down with flu and won't be in today."

"Consider it done, mate."

"When he's finished cursing, say I'll be back as soon as I can stagger. And there is one more thing. If Fleur rings and wants a word with me, explain I'm still on surveillance work and no one on the team is allowed to break away."

"Hullo, hullo, what's all this?"

"I don't want her to think I'm feeling as rotten as I am."

"You're a bloody liar and all power to your elbow – or wherever. As I always say, there's more than enough pebbles on the beach to fill one's pockets, so keep on bending down until one can't get it up any more."

Twenty-Two

A basic rule of detection taught at initial training was, start at the beginning, not in the middle. A far more complex requirement than it at first appeared since it was not always easy, or indeed possible, to identify what was the beginning of a train of events or the point from which all consequences flowed. In this case, however, the first thing to do was clearly to check whether Edwin Hastings lived in the Port de Majerda area. Within minutes of his arrival by taxi from the airport, Ballard went into a bar which overlooked water and had a large sign 'English is spoke', ordered a gin and tonic, and asked to borrow a telephone directory to look up the number of a friend of his.

He sat at a table, protected from the scorching sun by a multi-coloured umbrella, surrounded by tourists who seemed determined to drown both their sorrows and themselves as quickly as possible, and checked through the pages for E. Hastings. There was no entry. Then, largely by chance, he discovered that whilst entries were listed alphabetically, the whole area was not treated as one but was split up into towns so that all he had done so far was check that no E. Hastings lived in the provincial capital. He needed to remember that things were done differently in Spain. He found the Port de Majerda pages. There was one E. Hastings listed. He made a note of the address, handed the directory back and ordered a second gin and tonic.

* * *

167

Although Port de Majerda was largely known for the luxurious homes which lined the canals and the expensive boats tied up alongside, in the past years there had been such extensive development that by now by far the majority of houses lay inland from the canals; most of these provided holiday accommodation and were not intended for round-the-year living, but some were larger if seldom luxurious. When the taxi drew up in front of Tres Vencejos, Ballard saw a small bungalow with, at one end, a Catalan-style rock-faced tower, set in a plot of no more than fifteen hundred square metres. Common sense said that a man whose income placed him in the multimillionaire class would not live in such relatively mean accommodation, but imagination suggested he might give that as his address as a form of camouflage.

Ballard asked the taxi driver to wait, an unwelcome request, crossed the pavement and walked up the short paved path to the glass front door that was protected by a metal bar door that was swung back. He rang the bell. After a while, a man wearing shorts and with a beer belly opened the glass door. "Mr Hastings?"

"That's me last time I asked."

"Keith Lock suggested I called to have a word with you."

"Who's that, mate?"

"Detective Inspector Keith Lock."

"Wouldn't know him. I'm particular about who my friends are!" He guffawed at his own wit.

Camouflage could only be taken so far. This buffoon could never run a successful mob at a distance. "Then I've been given the wrong address. Very sorry to have bothered you."

"No real bother. There's not been much drinking time lost."

Ballard returned to the taxi. Some villains who escaped to Spain for a life of sun, sea, sangria, and if not in their overripe years, sex, did not bother to change their names, confident that they could beat extradition; others, not so certain, or arrogant, arrived with new names and all necessary supporting documents. It was impossible to guess what name Edwin Hastings might have adopted. There was, however, a further means of identifying him – the yacht. Ballard asked the driver to take him to the harbour master's office, a request that was eventually understood.

The harbour master, short, round, and more friendly than a typical Catalan, understood English until it became obvious that Ballard had come to ask questions, not pay mooring fees.

"I'm looking for this yacht."

The harbour master inspected his well-manicured nails.

"Do you have a list of names of all the yachts here?"

He shrugged his shoulders a second time.

"Will there be tax records showing who owns what yachts?"

There was now a puzzled expression on his face. Did this Englishman really imagine all the owners of yachts paid the taxes the state said they should?

Ballard thanked the other for his help, hoping his sarcasm would translate, left the office and went down the concrete steps to the quayside. He looked across the basin. At a guess, in this one were thirty to forty yachts amongst the motor cruisers. It was going to be a long, hot job . . .

Doe left the BMW bike behind a battered saloon and, carrying a holdall, walked up the pavement, moving carefully because the darkened reflective visor reduced the visibility from the street lighting; he had a fear of tripping and breaking a limb. As he moved, the two grenades, attached to a belt under the leathers, jiggled against his waist in time to his stride.

He opened the wooden gate of the end terrace house and entered the tiny garden. As he walked up to the front door, he noted the crude stained-glass fanlight and thought how odd it was that people who lived in houses such as this invariably lacked the taste even of a Philistine. He put the holdall down, brought out the spray can from his left-hand pocket and a small lead-filled cosh from his right-hand one. He turned, visually to check the road – a car drove past and then there was no traffic; on the far side, a couple were walking away from him. He rang the bell.

Through the opaque glass he saw the shadow of an approaching person. He rested his forefinger very lightly on the spray button.

"Who is it?"

Judging by the speaker's voice, the man was middle-aged to old, which meant there was less likelihood of a large family. "Sergeant Withers, local CID." The middle aged or old who lived in this kind of a house would always respond to the voice of authority without stopping to try to judge its authenticity.

He heard the sounds of a chain being withdrawn, then the sharp click of a lock snapping open. The door was drawn back. In front of him, scant grey hair framed by an overhead light, was a man in his middle sixties, already beginning to bow to age. He aimed the can and pressed the button in one smooth movement. As the spray hit the man's face, there was a second of total confusion, then he began frantically to paw at his eyes as he gasped. Doe brought the cosh down on the exposed neck with expert force. The man collapsed to the floor.

"Who is it, Dad?" came the call through the open doorway of the room to the right.

He moved close to the wall and waited.

"Dad, are you all right?"

She was beginning to worry; worried people became careless.

There were sounds of movement, the door was opened fully and a woman, plump to the point of fat, with the soft features of an even-tempered person, stepped into the narrow passage. She saw her husband inert on the floor and her face expressed shock as she started to look up at Doe. He used the spray, then the cosh. She lay in an untidy heap on the floor alongside her husband, her skirt flaring up to reveal enough of her thighs to have gravely embarrassed her had she been conscious.

The only sounds inside the house were those of the television. He was in luck, he thought as he retrieved the holdall from outside and closed the front door. But an intelligent man always made certain. A quick search showed that no one else was present. When he returned to the hall/passage both man and woman were deeply unconscious, but their breathing was sufficiently regular to suggest he had not injured them too severely. He tore strips off her cotton frock and used these to bind and gag them.

Carrying the holdall, he passed through the kitchen, unlocked the outside door, and went into the back garden. There was little fallout from the street lighting and everything was in as much darkness as was ever found in town. He stripped off leathers and helmet and placed them by the side of the holdall, from which he brought a ladder, made from strong cord and thin steel rods, which had two hooks at one end; he unfolded this and was able, just, to fix the hooks on the top of the wall. Climbing the ladder was difficult; to gain a foothold, he had to force the rungs away from the wall, but his own weight tried to hold them against it. He quickly learned to use his toes to take his weight, even though the unusual pressure was painful.

With his head above the level of the wall, he studied the very large garden beyond through the three strands of razor wire. There were ground lights, carefully placed so that their flat beams illuminated any approach to the house. A pair of dogs – probably Rottweilers, but he knew little about dogs – appeared from around the house and wandered aimlessly. He could not identify any surveillance cameras or movement detectors, but was convinced they would be there somewhere.

He used a compass to determine whether electricity was flowing through any of the strands of razor wire which were

fixed to angled struts; the compass needle did not react, showing it was not.

He brought a plastic bag out of a trouser pocket; this
contained a dozen cubes of meat which had been doped and
he threw these into the garden, then used a silent whistle to
attract the dogs' attention. They loped over and at first – to
his silent contempt – failed to mark the meat, but one of them
finally did and put its head down, advanced a couple of paces,
sniffed, ate; its companion followed suit. He descended to the
ground and walked around as he waited, trying to ease the pain
in the balls of his feet and his toes. He had been assured that
the dope would work within five minutes; one piece of meat
for each dog would have been enough, so if each had eaten
several, in six or seven minutes they would be dead. He was
very sorry he had had to make so certain that both dogs were
incapacitated that it had been necessary to use many lures; he
loved animals.

After ten minutes, he climbed back up the ladder, high
enough this time to use a pair of specially hardened cutters
to sever each strand of razor wire. He sat on the wall, pulled up
the ladder, dropped it over the other side after making certain
the hooks were well bedded.

He climbed down the ladder and crossed a gravel path and
then lawn, not running, but hurrying, because however slowly
those inside reacted to an alarm, eventually they'd decide to
treat it as genuine. He made for a window from which light
streamed out because curtains had not been drawn and stood at
the edge of the light to look into the room in which he'd been
just over a month before. Cairns was seated in one chair, Ronnie
in another; Osman was in the doorway, his attitude suggesting
he'd come to report the alarm. Remembering the contempt with
which Osman had treated him, Doe felt the gods were being
generous. He unhooked one Mills bomb from his belt and,
gripping the lever, pulled the pin free. He released the lever to

a snap of sound. He silently said, "And one," to reduce the fuse time to two seconds, lobbed the bomb through the window. He fell to the ground, in the cover of the house wall.

There was an explosion which hurt his eardrums and a blast of burning air above him; as his hearing returned, there were the sounds of objects hitting the ground. He came to his feet and ran, so unaccustomed to the exertion that he was panting by the time he reached the wall. He climbed the ladder, lifted it and set it on the other side, descended until his head was just above the level of the wall. Small tongues of flame were reaching out of the room, now otherwise in darkness, and in the garden lights he could see some of the debris littering the previously immaculate path and lawn. There was no pursuer.

He descended to the ground, unhooked the ladder after a brief struggle, rolled it up and placed it in the holdall. He pulled on leathers and helmet, went into the house. Both man and woman seemed to be recovering consciousness, but it would be some time before they could move and summon help so, enjoying this chance to lessen their distress, he released their bonds and removed the gags. As he went through to the front door, the remaining Mills bomb jiggled against his waist. Things had gone so smoothly that it had not been needed to delay pursuers. A thousand pounds spent unnecessarily.

There were no people in the road, excitedly asking what had happened. As he opened the gate and walked along the pavement to the motor bike he wondered if their television sets had been playing too loudly for them to have heard the explosion; or had they, since they had not in any way been harmed, decided to leave someone else to find out what was the trouble? Altruism was not a flourishing flower in modern suburbia.

He knew excited tension as he started the engine and drove away. It was not the sound of a police car siren which caused this, but the thought of Audrey; red hair and expensive, she promised delights to match imagination.

173

Twenty-Three

B allard spent much of Sunday morning in a small dinghy
with temperamental outboard sailing along the main
canals which were deep enough for larger yachts. It was hot
and eventually tiring work because it seemed less and less likely
to bear any result; his thoughts were on long, ice-cool drinks
and piquant food when he saw a blue-hulled yacht moored at
the foot of a sloping lawn.

He throttled back and the outboard coughed, spluttered, and
died. He swore. Ten pulls on the starter failed to restore life
and it seemed he'd either have to row back, only there were
no oars, or abandon ship, when on the eleventh pull of the cord
the engine started again. He sailed slowly along, comparing
the yacht in front of him with the description he'd been given
in Gransere. A yawl – which research had told him was a
two-masted fore-and-aft boat with the mizzen-mast stepped far
aft – blue hull, low deckhead, in first-class condition with fresh
varnish, polished brass, new rigging . . .

The grounds behind the yacht were comparatively large and
the sloping lawn was almost up to bowling-green standard; the
several flower beds were filled with colour. Beyond the lawn
was a large U-shaped bungalow, to the right of which was a
swimming pool, to the left, a hard tennis court. Having noted the
prices of property in estate agents' advertisements, he reckoned
this place would probably be worth close to a million pounds.
The kind of place a rich villain would choose to live in . . .

As the port side of the yacht's stern became visible, he read the name, *Harold*. So the owner was probably British or perhaps Norwegian – or did they spell the name Harald? . . . Was his brain in the deep freeze? Harold had fought and died in the battle of Hastings and Edwin Hastings had a sense of humour . . . Against all the odds, he had succeeded! And yet he enjoyed no sense of triumph. Lock was a traitor.

All that remained was to gain a sight of the occupants of the house and identify Hastings from the mug shot he had brought from England.

Hastings appeared to many to be a man of contradictions because they failed to realise that beneath his pleasant manner was someone who saw the world through totally selfish eyes. He could be friendly, yet never if this might cost him; he would help people who were in trouble, yet saw murder as the best solution for those who troubled him; he despised drug addicts, yet fuelled their addictions; he loved his son and daughter, yet encouraged the exploitation of young women and men, girls and boys, in prostitution and pornography; he held loyalty to be a necessary virtue, yet would show great disloyalty if this would benefit him.

He dressed casually, in clothes that bore the stamp of expensive quality, and took great care over his appearance; he was a compulsive purchaser of lotions and creams which promised younger skin. He respected and honoured his wife and so made certain she was never embarrassed by meeting his current mistresses. He sent his son to Rugby and his daughter to L'Academie de Rijon in Switzerland where she was quickly learning to be a snob. He gave lavish parties where guests ate food and drank champagne they could not afford for themselves. He showed compassion by supporting very generously a local association which helped British expatriates who ran into financial trouble. In England, he could have passed as a modern gentleman.

He was sitting in the shade of an overhead sunblind when Phelan came round the corner of the house. "Need a word," Phelan said in the harsh voice of someone who smoked very heavily.

Virginia stood. "I'd better check the meal." She was very careful not to know anything about her husband's business.

"Don't forget the Pickerings are here for lunch," Hastings said.

She smiled. "They're not people one forgets."

He watched her walk across to the doorway and go inside. She had style and elegance; she made most of the local female expats look like sacks of potatoes. He turned to Phelan. "Help yourself to a drink."

"Thanks, boss." Phelan went across to the refrigerated drinks trolley and poured out a generous brandy, added ginger ale and three cubes of ice. He sat on the patio chair that Virginia had recently vacated.

"Is there a problem?"

"I ain't sure. But there could be."

"Name it."

"I was doing some cleaning in the for'd cabin when I looked through the port and saw a dinghy come upstream real slowly; so slowly, I wondered what was up and kept watching. The bloke in it was giving the yacht a real once-over."

"There's nothing unusual in that. There's not another yacht in the place to match her."

"Sure. But he wasn't like an ordinary tourist. He . . . Difficult to explain, boss. I kept watching. He continued upstream for a little, turned about, and checked the yacht again as he came past. Got a bit downstream and increased speed and was away."

"So?"

"I reckon he was a split."

"Unlikely."

"Maybe. But that's what he was. I can smell 'em."

Hastings accepted 'smell' in the sense intended – the ability to identify a detective by instinct as much as by any visible signs of an unusual alertness. He drained his glass. "Get me another gin and tonic."

Phelan, showing no resentment at being treated as a servant, put his glass down, stood, collected the other's glass, and refilled it at the drinks trolley. "How many ice?"

"Four. Have you seen this man before?"

"No." Phelan handed the glass to Hastings, sat.

"What age?"

"Middle twenties. White faced, so he's newly out from home. Built like he can handle himself."

"Anything more?"

"Only that the dinghy looked like it was one of them what's hired out."

"Find out if it was."

Phelan drained his glass, stood. "I could be wrong, but I don't reckon to be."

Hastings stared at the canal, the surface of which was being rippled by the lightest of breezes so that the sun's reflection shimmered. A simple tourist? Many of them sailed down the canal and all who did admired his yacht. But Phelan was steady and if he claimed a man was a split, it was odds on he was.

The Pickerings were typical ex-army – after the third pink gin, he'd explain at length why the force had deteriorated after he'd stood down, she was the colonel's lady and even when cold sober believed herself to be the arbiter on all matters social. Hastings considered them to be bores, but useful because they were regarded by many of the expatriates – the natural rankers of the world – to be important people. In addition, their snobbish stupidity appealed to his sense of humour.

After his second post-luncheon cognac, Pickering expressed his considered opinion that General Montgomery hadn't known his arse from his elbow and then regarded his empty balloon glass with a thirsty look. Hastings was about to suggest he allowed himself a third cognac, when the younger maid entered the drawing room, crossed to where he sat, and in a low voice said, in her weird mixture of Catalan and English, that Señor Phelan wished to speak to him. He excused himself and went out, leaving a disgruntled guest.

Phelan was in the television room. "I found an outfit what hired out a dinghy to a bloke what fits the description. He asked 'em if they knew a yawl with a blue hull."

Hastings stared through the picture window at the sloping lawn and the yacht, part of her upperworks glinting in the sunlight. No casual tourist. Probably the smart bastard of a split who'd caused endless trouble already. Lock had mentioned – almost certainly inadvertently – his name on one occasion. What had that been? Something to do with singing? . . . Why did one's mind so often go walkabout when most needed?

How threatened was he? He was living under an assumed name and had all the necessary papers and documents to support that, but this defence had now been breached. Highly paid lawyers in England had assured him that as matters stood there could be no question of his being extradited from Spain; highly paid Spanish lawyers had confirmed that. But if he were linked to the murders of Jenner and Cairns, then extradition was certain. And however pressed, Lock wouldn't be able to do anything for him . . .

He came to a stop in the middle of the carpet. "Go back to the hire firm and find out if they can give you any more info about this bloke."

"Boss, they can't. I questioned 'em all ways."

"Find out."

Phelan crossed to the door.

Abruptly, perhaps because he wasn't now trying to remember the name, he did. "Cool it."

Phelan turned.

"His name's Ballard and he'll be staying at one of the hotels. You and Les check out which one."

Phelan left, closed the door behind himself.

Hastings resumed his pacing. Ballard would visually have to identify him – Patrick Stevens – as Edwin Hastings before he could be certain. When he'd drifted past in the dinghy, he hadn't had the chance to do that. So now he would probably keep watch on the house, perhaps from the other side of the canal . . .

Doe was due in a couple of hours to collect the final tranche of the hit money. As a man, Hastings held him in even greater contempt than most, but as an assassin, in the greatest respect.

He returned to the drawing room. "Sorry to leave you like that, but there was a small problem which had to be sorted out."

Pickering fiddled with his empty glass. "As I always told my juniors, the only way to deal with a problem is to face it head on and smack it dead."

"I think I'd agree with that . . . Can I possibly tempt you to another cognac?"

"Don't mind if I do, so long as it's not too big, as the actress said to the bishop."

"Reginald!" snapped his wife, who never let him forget that his grandfather had been a grocer while hers had been a baronet.

Twenty-Four

Aparthotel Pirineos was on the southern outskirts of Port de Majerda, a kilometre and a half back from the seafront. Built around a large open space, in the centre of which was a swimming pool, it offered apartments of one or two bedrooms, each with a small sitting room, kitchen, shower room, and lavatory; for those who did not want to cook, there was a restaurant, for those who welcomed company, a lounge.

In the lounge, Ballard mentally struggled with the problem, to ring or not to ring Fleur? If he did, there'd be no immediate way in which she'd be able to judge he was in Spain and not on a surveillance job in the county, but when he spoke to her, love often confused his tongue and he might so easily say something that would alert her . . .

"I say, do you speak English?"

"Yes," he answered, annoyed by the unwelcome interruption. He looked up at a man whose face offered no immediate impression of character.

"I thought you must be British, but one can make a mistake; sometimes, a German can look very British. Wouldn't you agree?"

"Can't say I've ever thought about it."

"And you're just out from home, aren't you? D'you mind if I sit?" He sat. "One can usually tell by the pale skin. After even a couple of days out here, one starts to brown."

"Really." He hoped his plonking tone would discourage the other.

"It's truly amazing what the sun has done for this country. If it had our weather at home, the tourist industry would be only a fraction of what it is now and the country would have remained poor . . ."

His mind returned to the problem as the puerile words continued. To phone or not to phone; that is the question: Whether 'tis kinder for the mind to suffer, The slings and arrows of outrageous truth, Or to use silence against a sea of pain . . . There was a more immediate silence and he realised he'd been asked a question. "I'm sorry, I didn't quite catch that." He wondered why one was so often polite when rudeness would be more to the point.

"I was wondering if this was your first visit to Port de Majerda?"

"Yes, it is."

"Then I'm certain you'll enjoy every minute . . . But we're talking away and are still strangers! My name's John Doe."

Here was one man whose name suited him perfectly. A nobody. If required to describe the other, he'd have had great difficulty in doing so in meaningful terms. Ears were categorised as Darwinian extensions, Darwinian tubercle, frostbitten, and so on, but Doe's were just shapeless humps . . .

"And you are?"

"Geoffrey Ballard."

"Very nice to meet you, Geoffrey."

At least it hadn't been, 'Pleased to meet you.'

"Are you here on your own?"

"Yes."

"But maybe not for very long!"

"How d'you mean?"

"I'm sorry, I was being rather stupid, wasn't I? It's just that there are lots of lovely young ladies on the beaches. But perhaps they wouldn't interest you?"

If this was a come-on, Doe was going to learn his mistake very, very sharply.

"I say, would you like a drink?"

"No, thanks."

"The locals have a saying, 'A drink before the meal is like lace underwear.' They mean, it stimulates the appetite."

"Really."

"I'd say it's not stimulation that most expats need! I know one chap – made his money in cars – who boasts that in the summer he has five different bedfellows a week."

For the first time, Ballard was interested in what the other was saying. "Do you know many of the British who live here?"

"I'd say, almost all of them. Things are different from home, you'll understand, and it doesn't matter where you went to school or what job you had, any of that sort of thing. I suppose it's because there aren't all that number of British here and people are much more ready to mix. Of course, there are a few snobs. Just as there are a few one really doesn't want to know."

"Do you mind if I change my mind and have a drink?"

"Couldn't be more delighted. So what will it be?"

"I'll shout." Ballard stood.

"That's very friendly of you. A vodka and tonic, if that's all right?"

Was he so gormless he needed permission to choose a drink? Ballard crossed to the far end of the lounge where there was a small bar, tended by a young man who ogled every female between fifteen and fifty. As he waited, Ballard thought of the fruitless hours he had spent watching the house and yacht, yet now, by chance, there was the possibility of finding out what he needed to know. Life moved more in ironic ways, than mysterious.

He carried the glasses back to the table. Doe raised his. "May your life be happy, whether long or short."

An odd toast. From an odd man. "I take it you live here?"

"First came several years ago and had the dream of retiring here. It's good to have dreams, isn't it?"

"So they say."

"You never really expect them to come true, so when they do, it's like . . . I don't know what it's like. Just out of this world. You see, the way things happened for me was that I had a sister who married very well. She wanted children, but couldn't have any, and then her husband died quite young. We grew closer together even though we didn't see each other all that often – of course, we phoned a lot – and then she was tragically killed in a car crash. It seems some families are destined for bad luck, as if under a curse . . . But I'm not going to burden you with my miseries. You'll have enough of your own. My sister named me as her sole beneficiary in her will and so I inherited everything. I was surprised how much that was. It enabled me to retire immediately and come out here to live. A dream come true."

"You're very fortunate."

"Don't I know that! I enjoy myself doing what I like best. How many people can claim that?"

"Very few back home. But surely most of the expatriates here have a great life?"

"A lot of them are always complaining about something. I often wonder why they stay here."

"Judging by some of the yachts, there's serious money around?"

"I call myself very comfortably off, but there are some here who'd tell you I must almost be on my uppers! You've just mentioned yachts. Jack – a good friend – has a relatively small one and he told me what that's cost him over five years. Unbelievable! He says there's always something needs doing. He's even had a problem with the hull that's made of fibreglass, or something very similar – the salt water seeped in and bubbled it. Repairs cost him thousands of pounds. Or millions of pesetas."

"I saw a beautiful yacht this morning when I was sailing around the canals."

"I wonder whose that was."

"She looked so smart she maybe has just been built. Paintwork was immaculate, brasswork shining, and the ropes could have been blancoed."

"Where was this?"

"In one of the main canals."

"I don't suppose you can remember the colour of the hull?"

"Dark blue."

"And was it tied up in front of a large house with a swimming pool and a hard tennis court?"

"As a matter of fact, yes, she was. Do you know the one I'm talking about, then?"

"I'll bet you were looking at Patrick's yacht. I've been out in it a couple of times; just for the day, of course."

"Presumably, he's one of the rich?"

"He employs two or three locals in the house and the garden and when you know what the Spanish welfare taxes are, you know he has to be very, very rich."

"Made his fortune in England and retired out here to spend it?"

"Something like that, I suppose, though I don't know what his business was. Never talks about that, which seems strange when one stops to think about it because most of 'em never stop telling you what they did and how successful they were."

According to the records, Edwin Hastings had a wife, a son, and a daughter. "Is he married?"

"To one of the nicest persons you could hope to meet. There are some women who never let you forget how rich they are, but she's not a bit like that. And I know for a fact that more than once she's helped out people here who've run into money problems. The rich don't usually do that sort of thing. I say, that's why they're rich."

Ballard obligingly chuckled. "Does he have a family?"

"A boy and a girl. As I remember, the girl's at a very posh finishing school in Switzerland. Didn't know that sort of place still existed until Patrick told me . . . Oh, dear!"

"There's a problem?"

"Is that really the time?"

Ballard looked at the electric clock on the wall, then at his wristwatch. "Dead on."

"Then I'm terribly sorry, I must rush. It's been so interesting talking to you, I've lost all count of the time. I'm due at the Sopworths for lunch and they become very irritable if anyone arrives late. That's really rather silly because time in Spain is so elastic, but they are very set in their ways." He stood. "I feel guilty."

"About arriving late?"

"At not returning your very kind hospitality. Will you let me buy you another drink at the bar and tell them to bring it over to you?"

"There's no need."

"But I was brought up in the belief that it's a sin to receive and not give . . . I tell you what, let me buy you a drink tomorrow?"

"That sounds a good idea."

"Let's say, here at twelve?"

"OK by me."

"Great. So it's goodbye until tomorrow." He left and took a couple of paces, then turned back. "I've had a better idea. You can't know the area as it's your first visit, so let me show you a little of it and you can see how attractive the countryside is. And we could have lunch at my favourite restaurant."

"Sounds a good idea."

"A lot of French eat there and I think that's always a sign of good food."

"An infallible one."

"Then that's settled. Goodbye, Geoffrey, until twelve tomorrow." He finally left.

If, Ballard thought, the little man knew so many local compatriots, why had he been very keen to talk to a stranger? It was odds-on that the majority of expats regarded him with indifference. But he could have his uses for a newcomer. Tomorrow he might confirm or deny that Patrick was in truth Edwin Hastings.

Ballard picked up his glass and went over to the bar, asked for another gin and tonic. He wondered how surprised and shaken Doe would be if told he had been speaking to a detective who was now seeking to find the proof that his superior was a traitor.

Twenty-Five

Ballard used a handkerchief to wipe the sweat from his forehead, face, and neck. If there was a more uncomfortable task than keeping watch from a hired car in the baking sun, he didn't want to undertake it. He wondered how he could have lacked the foresight to buy a bottle of water and a bag of ice from the insulated cabinet outside the petrol station; why all the occupants of the house had chosen to stay indoors; why time was elastic and stretched whenever one wished it to shorten; why he'd persuaded himself that it was necessary to try to catch sight of Patrick Stevens when there was every chance that what he learned during the coming lunch would prove this to be unnecessary?

At a quarter past twelve, having seen only the gardener, he left his viewing point and drove off, crossing a bridge over a wide canal and then along roads lined with bungalows and houses which became smaller the further from the seafront.

Doe was waiting in the lounge of the aparthotel even though it was not yet five to the hour. "Good morning, Geoffrey. It's a lovely day, isn't it?"

That depended on how one had spent it so far. "Sure. Is it OK with you if we wait to take off until I've had a drink? My throat's like the Sahara."

"Of course. And it's my turn."

"But Dutch from then on."

"I was hoping you'd let me buy the lunch as I live here."

187

"Thanks all the same, but it's Dutch or we go hungry."

"I'd rather not do that," Doe said very earnestly. "They cook garlic chicken better than anywhere else I've ever eaten . . . What would you like to drink now?"

"A gin and tonic, please."

Ballard sat. There was no need to rush things and he'd wait to start the questions until after lunch, having made certain Doe drank well beforehand; with luck, the other would have lost guard of his tongue and would not wonder why a stranger should be so interested in the very rich Patrick Stevens . . . Early on, he'd had the photo of Hastings computer-copied, but was still undecided whether to show it to Doe. To do so would produce a direct answer, but it might provoke dangerous interest if Doe, clearly not tight-lipped, mentioned the incident to Hastings. But if identification was made, surely Doe's curiosity would be immaterial? He, Ballard, would return to England, finally certain Lock was a traitor. What happened then would be for others to decide . . .

Doe returned, passed him a glass, sat. "Have you been swimming?"

If he were the typical tourist he claimed to be, he would have done. He answered that he'd spent a long time in the water.

"You want to be very careful about the sun, you know. There's not much pollution in the air here and it can be really strong. When I see people sunbathing until their skin is lobster red, I worry."

"Why? That's up to them."

"But often people don't stop and think and it can be a kindness to remind them."

"When it's ten to one they treat the reminder as an insult?"

"You're a cynic!"

"A realist."

"A cynical realist." Doe chuckled. "I hope you aren't offended by my little joke?"

188

Did the other ever stop apologising? "Of course not."

Doe checked the time. "I don't like to rush you, but I think perhaps we should move. I phoned the restaurant and booked a table, but if they are very busy, they sometimes forget reservations and when we turn up, we might have to wait."

Ballard drained his glass.

"I do hope the meal is good. I'd feel so upset if it isn't, having persuaded you to go there."

"For the record, I won't hold you personally responsible."

Doe laughed.

Ballard was briefly intrigued by the strange quality he seemed to catch in the other's laughter and wondered what, if anything, this signified. Just a sign of nerves on the part of someone who half accepted his colourless insignificance?

Doe drove around the countryside for a while, pointing out various places of interest, then turned on to the autoroute and continued on this almost to the French border before leaving it to head northwards into hilly country that quickly became mountainous.

As the road became ever more twisty, Doe drove ever more slowly. A light van came behind them and hooted twice, then pulled out to overtake; as the driver drew level, he held up one finger to show his contempt for such careful progress.

"How dangerous to overtake me there," Doe said, as he rounded the sharp corner. "If a car had been coming downhill, there could have been a terrible crash. As I always say, one can't be too careful. I mean, after the meal are we just going to drive peacefully back to the aparthotel?"

"It's to be hoped so," Ballard answered drily.

"But we can't be certain that something won't prevent us both reaching there, can we?"

"I suppose not."

"Are you glad you can't see into the future?"

"I'll answer that if you can tell me what's going to happen."

"Suppose I told you that sometimes I can?"

"I'll ask for the winning numbers of next week's Lottery."

"I can't ever tell that sort of thing. But sometimes . . ." He braked to go round a right-hand hairpin bend. "Sometimes I have a precognition concerning someone. I don't tell them, of course."

"Why not?"

"It's so often unpleasant and I don't want to upset them."

"If you did, he could take steps to avoid whatever unpleasantness you reckon's going to overtake him."

"You can't avoid the future."

Ballard made no further comment. It was a pointless conversation.

After a while, Doe said: "Have you noticed the trees on your right? They're cork trees and a section of their trunks are smooth because they were harvested last year. Patrick Stevens was talking about buying part of an oak forest that's up for sale. I haven't heard if he's made up his mind yet."

Since Doe had brought up the name, there could be no harm in showing mild curiosity. "He must be as rich as you suggested, then?"

"He is."

"So how did he make his bundle?"

"Like I said yesterday, I don't really know. He never talks about his business, but someone did once try to suggest that it was a bit shady. I don't believe that, of course – I'll bet the person concerned was making it up because of jealousy. There's a lot of that, even amongst the rich who you wouldn't think had cause to be jealous of anyone."

"Where did he live before he came out here?"

"Up north somewhere; he has told me exactly where, but I can't remember." They reached the end of a short stretch of relatively straight road and Doe braked. "We're nearly there. Are you hungry?"

190

"Yes."

"I always try to be hungry. Do you know why?"

"I've no idea."

"Then I eat a really good meal. That's important when you remember the saying, 'Let us eat and drink, for tomorrow we shall die.'"

"Seems to me to be rather a counter-productive spur to hunger."

"But it can be so true. One should always take one's pleasures while one can."

"Certain there will be more to come."

"I can see you're a real optimist."

"Yesterday, I was a cynic."

"A cynical optimist!"

They turned another corner to come in sight of houses built higgledy-piggledy around the crest of a low mountain.

Doe drove into a parking area. "We have to stop here because cars aren't allowed in the village; only donkey carts. You don't see many of those these days, but when I first came here, there seemed to be more carts than cars." He braked to a halt. "Have you noticed all the French-registered cars here? It's only a few kilometres to the border and the French drive across for a better and cheaper meal than they'd get at home."

"They'd never admit to such heresy."

Doe laughed.

Too easily amused; trying hard to flatter in order to be suffered? Ballard stepped out of the car into a breeze which provided a welcome coolness.

"On the other side of the village, there's a view right across to the sea and if the air's really clear, down a fair way to the south. You might like to have a look after the meal?" he suggested, as he activated the remote locking.

"It's an idea."

"We could do that now, but I think we ought to go straight

to the restaurant with so many people here, to judge by all the cars." He looked at his watch. "We're almost exactly on time, but one never knows."

"Even with your powers of precognition?"

Doe's laughter was louder than before. "What a sense of humour you have, Geoffrey!"

They walked along the narrow road that rose at an ever steeper incline. "I've just remembered," Doe said. "I mean, where Patrick used to live in England. He showed me a photo of his house once. It looked big, but not quite a mansion, if you know what I mean? He said it was on the edge of a village called Hartley Gereham. That's a funny name."

A name which surely clinched the issue; Hastings had lived in Hartley Gereham before leaving England. Later, Ballard decided, he would show Doe the photograph and finally settle things.

They entered the village, the cobbled streets of which were almost all at different levels. The outside of the restaurant looked so unimpressive that Ballard decided they'd come to the Spanish equivalent of an English roadside caff.

Doe said: "I know it doesn't look much, but looks can be very deceptive, can't they?"

The other's tone made Ballard regard him, wondering whether there was some unexpected, hidden meaning behind his words, but his expression remained as colourlessly uninformative as ever.

Twenty-Six

"D'you like it?" Doe asked, after Ballard had eaten his first mouthful of Serano ham and melon; "I do hope yours is as tasty as mine," he said very earnestly over the garlic chicken; "Isn't it wonderfully smooth?" he said through a mouthful of chocolate mousse and Cointreau-flavoured whipped cream.

As the waitress handed him the bill, he said: "Well, was I right? Wasn't it delicious?"

"Very," Ballard replied briefly. He would have enjoyed the meal more if he hadn't been constantly called upon to testify to his enjoyment. "What's the total?"

"It's my privilege."

"We agreed earlier on that it would be Dutch."

"I'd so like to treat you."

Ballard remembered a boy at school, the butt of bullies, who'd constantly given away things to try to buy friendships. His tone was sharper than intended when he said: "Thanks, but it's Dutch. What's my half?"

"You're so forceful, Geoffrey!"

Gawd! he thought silently. The information he'd sought and gained was being dearly earned. "I always pay my dues."

"Then if you insist. The total is seven thousand five hundred."

"What do you add for a tip?"

"The locals hardly give anything, but I'm always generous because I think that helps to lessen resentment of foreigners. Don't you agree?"

"Sure. What do you call generous?"

"A thousand."

"Then you want four thousand two fifty."

"If you must insist. But I would so like it to be my treat."

Ballard passed across a two-thousand and two one-thousand peseta notes and several coins. Doe added a similar amount and put the money on top of the bill on the plate. "You'd like to see the view before we leave, wouldn't you?"

He'd have preferred to drive straight back to the aparthotel and divest himself of Doe's company, which was becoming more and more glutinous, but, giving in to the dictates of politeness, he said he would.

They left the restaurant and made their way along several cobbled roads to the point where the village abruptly ended at a rock face which dropped vertically for some ten metres – being Spain, there was little protection from this danger.

"Isn't it a divine view!" Doe declaimed.

Attractive, Ballard thought, but lacking divinity. To their left, the Pyrenees petered out; the plain ahead of them was patchworked with woods and beyond it was the distant glint of sea; to their right were serried rows of hills.

"You'll never see anything like this again!"

Doe had spoken with underlined certainty. The wine was talking, Ballard decided. "Shall we move?"

"You're in a hurry to get somewhere?"

"I can only enjoy a view for so long."

"You don't draw out your pleasures? I try always to prolong them."

They retraced their route through the village and down to the car park. If anything, Doe drove more slowly than on the ascent and Ballard thought of asking him if he was selfishly prolonging some pleasure peculiar to himself, but decided the question would lose its force because it would be taken seriously.

When they were on one of the steeper sections of road,

Doe braked to a stop. "I'm afraid I must stop. I need a leak."

As so often happened, especially after sharing a bottle and a half of wine, the suggestion triggered a need and Ballard got out of the car. They were above a valley a kilometre or more wide and trees stretched from where they were across the floor of the valley and halfway up the far mountain. Moving very carefully, they descended the slope until hidden from the road. Doe continued further down to go out of sight – presumably, Ballard decided scornfully, from an over-developed sense of prudery.

He had begun to climb back up to the road, stopped when Doe called out: "Geoffrey, come down here and see something you'll never see again."

A tree; a flower; an insect? Reluctantly, he turned back and with even greater care – since here the slope steepened – made his way down to a small clearing, littered with stones, in which grew only grass, wild chicory, and brambles. Doe stood on the far side, in the shadow of a pine tree, hands in pockets. Ballard came to a stop, seeing nothing unusual and wondering why Doe was looking at him with such strange intentness. "What's so special?"

"The sky, the trees, the grass."

"What's that supposed to mean?"

"Only what the words say."

Doe's tone perplexed Ballard. "Are you trying to be funny?"

"There have been one or two moments when I've been amused."

"By what?"

"The fact that reality has proved to be so different from popular myth."

"What myth?"

"That detectives are clever."

It was as if he'd been hit by a mental thunderbolt. Amidst

a turmoil of confusion, he finally understood some truths. All the time he'd been congratulating himself on fooling Doe, questioning him without his realising he was being questioned or why, it had been he – PC/DC Ballard – who was being taken for a sucker. That odd laughter, those phrases introduced at odd moments – 'Are you glad you can't see into the future?' '. . . looks can be very deceptive, don't you think?' 'You'll never see anything like this again!' '. . . see something you'll never see again.' – had been expressing a sadistic pleasure, not a glutinous, naive stupidity. What better camouflage for an assassin than a totally colourless personality? Why hadn't he remembered how impossible it had been for Marr to describe the man he'd seen leave the car and board the yacht?

Ballard knew a gut-wrenching fear, but also anger directed at himself for his own stupidity; the anger helped him to keep control of his fear.

The distance between them was too great to be able to cover it before Doe had time to withdraw the gun he undoubtedly had in his right pocket and fire. If he turned and ran, he could not make the cover of the surrounding trees before a bullet tore into his back. He was in a hopeless position. Yet Doe liked to prolong his pleasures and all the time he believed his victim hadn't understood the whole truth, he'd not act. Massage that one weakness while desperately trying to find a way of escape from the inescapable . . . "I don't understand. Why start talking about detectives?"

"You can't think why?"

"No."

"Come now, Geoffrey, surely you're not that unintelligent?"

"All right, I am one. But when I'm on holiday, I never tell anyone in case it makes them feel uncomfortable."

"And you thought the knowledge would make me feel uncomfortable?"

"It seemed possible."

"What a thoughtful man! Should I thank you?"

"Of course not . . . Shall we get going?"

"Perhaps one of us might as well."

"I don't want to cause offence, but I think it would be a good idea if I drove back to Majerda."

"Why's that?"

"I think you've had too much to drink."

"What leads you to that conclusion?"

"The way you're not making much sense." Ballard spoke very earnestly and gestured with his hands, to mask the fact that he was very slowly moving one step forward. "I don't know what the drink/drive laws are in Spain, but it looks as if alcohol hits you rather hard – you wouldn't want to be hauled up by the police and be breathalysed, would you?"

"You think I'm drunk?"

"Let's say, under the influence."

"Nevertheless, I'm afraid I'm going to be driving back."

"Why take the risk?"

"You've no idea?"

"Of course not."

"I wonder. Am I going to have to revise my opinion of you? Can anyone really be as dumb as you're trying to make out?"

"All I'm trying to do is help."

"You still don't appreciate that I was called in because you were trying to find out if Patrick Stevens was Edwin Hastings?"

"Who's Edwin Hastings?"

Doe laughed.

Ballard again gestured with his arms to draw attention away from the fact that he was moving forward. "I don't know anyone called Hastings." One more step and he would be close enough to risk . . .

"Now you can stay where you are," Doe said as he withdrew his right hand in which he held a small automatic. "That's close enough."

197

Close enough because any closer would become dangerous to Doe or close enough to make certain that the shot fired would be lethal when the weapon was a snub-nosed .22 that even in the hands of an expert lacked certain killing power at any distance because of inaccuracy? Doe had marked each move. Now, all that lay between life and death was pressure on the trigger. Was Doe feeding perverse pleasure by continuing to delay things? Then feeding that perversity was the only chance left . . . "I . . . I . . ." he stuttered, pitching his voice high.

"You . . . You . . . ?" Doe mocked.

"You can't do this."

He laughed.

"But why?"

"If you still can't work that out, I'd better aim for your heart because your head must be hollow."

"It'll be murder."

"I'd call it necessary homicide."

"No. You can't." Ballard dropped to his knees, rested his hands on the ground. "I beg you, in the name of God, don't. I'm getting married soon . . ."

"Rest assured your girlfriend will not have to suffer widow-hood."

"I'll give you all my money if you'll let me go."

"Have you any?"

"Yes."

"This could be becoming more interesting. Since I don't really want to kill you, perhaps we could do a deal. How much can you offer?"

"Two thousand."

"Two thousand!" Doe repeated scornfully. "I thought we were talking about real money."

"I'll never tell anyone what happened." Ballard moved his right arm as if needing to adjust his balance and his index finger touched a rounded stone, large enough if his aim was true.

Would it be? He'd been a good cricketer, but that was several years ago and then nothing more than his team's chances of winning the match had rested on the accuracy of his throw . . . "Suppose I could find a bit more?"

"Say, ten thousand?"

He edged the stone under his fingers and against the palm of his hand, came to his feet very slowly, even moving back half a pace as if too scared to think of active resistance. "I just haven't that sort of money."

"What a pity – your company's given me great pleasure."

Doe seemed to be enjoying the situation so much that he had noticed nothing. But Ballard had thought this before and been proved wrong. "Perhaps the bank will give me a personal loan for the extra money."

"They'll need security, being bloodsuckers. Do you own a house?"

"Yes."

Doe chuckled. "You're a liar, Geoffrey. You live in a rented flat. Naughty, trying to tell me porkies! Shall I let you into a little secret? Even if you could come up with a hundred thousand, you'd be wasting your breath."

"Why?"

"I'm contracted. I always honour my contract."

He altered his stance to gain a better balance for the throw. "How much are you being paid to kill me?"

"Too much, since it's so easy. I don't suppose you can understand this, Geoffrey, but I've pride in my work which means I like a job to be difficult because then afterwards I can know there's no one else who would have been able to do it. But you're so dumb, you're anyone's target."

"If you kill me, you'll be arrested because I left a note at the aparthotel to be opened if I don't return."

"Because you were suspicious of me? You can be a right comedian! D'you reckon I'm still at my mother's tits? You didn't begin to sus what was going on until I pulled this gun and even then it's taken you time to understand; and like as not, you still can't really work it all out." He laughed as he looked up at the sky, perhaps calling on the gods to share his amusement for this fool.

Ballard threw the stone. It struck Doe on the right cheek-bone, fracturing it, and sending him momentarily off balance. Instinctively, he raised his right hand towards his cheek where pain was exploding, forgetting he was holding the gun.

Ballard threw himself forward in a committed tackle that would have impressed an All Black, slammed into Doe's legs above the knees with the force to fling the other to the ground. Doe, showing far more resilience that his appearance suggested he could possess, brought the automatic down and fired. The bullet missed Ballard and ricocheted with an angry whine, the hot blast from the muzzle singed Ballard's flesh. He grabbed Doe's wrist and wrenched it upwards as a second shot was fired; the branch of a tree snapped off and fell to the ground. He brought up his right knee and there was a scream of pain, but Doe retained sufficient control of his senses to drop the gun and catch it in his other hand. Ballard let go of the right wrist, frantically grabbed for the left one before the gun could be brought round and down. For a second they strained against each other, then abruptly his greater strength overcame Doe's resistance and turned the wrist inwards with such force and at such an angle that the trigger was inadvertently pulled. The sound of the shot was muffled because the muzzle was in Doe's side. He made a sound that was part cry, part unenunciated word. His eyes expressed pain, but also a puzzled incomprehension – how could he, an expert, have been bested by a naive incompetent? Blood began to trickle out of the corner of his mouth, to match the blood that was staining his shirt where the bullet had entered. He tried to raise his right hand, began to drum his heels on the ground. Then he died.

In his work, Ballard had seen death frequently, but never before been present at its arrival. It was a shocking experience, made worse not only by his part in its coming, but also reaction from the knowledge that it could so easily have been he who lay there. He thought he was going to be sick. A bluebottle buzzed around the dead man's mouth and he aimed a wild swipe at it and missed. It returned and this time he did not bother to disturb it.

He struggled to overcome shock, nausea, reaction, and to think coherently. He was in a foreign country in the company of a man for whose death he was partially responsible. How could he prove self-defence? The questions were obvious. How long had he known Doe? Why had their friendship apparently been so rapid? Had the attraction been sexual? Had Doe been trying to fend off his advances? . . . He remembered reading that a suspect in Spain could be held in jail for months, perhaps even years, before his trial was held . . .

Clearly, Doe had lured him to the present spot to kill him because it was somewhere where his body was unlikely to be discovered before it had decomposed – and in the hot summer this would be soon – to the point where identification could be so time and resources consuming that without specific reason for it no attempt would be made. So if he stripped the body and removed all means of identification, it almost certainly would ensure anonymity . . . But he was a police officer, sworn to promote the law; almost certainly, an attempt to hide a violent death was a criminal offence under Spanish law.

He wasn't conscious of reaching a decision, yet he stripped off Doe's cotton shirt, trousers (in the back pocket of which was a wallet), pants, socks, shoes, wristwatch, and heavy gold ring. As he stared down at the nude body, with a very small, puckered wound that had a narrow trial of drying blood leading from it, he seemed to have become two persons – one who did and one who observed . . .

He dragged the body to the edge of the clearing, at which point the ground fell away precipitously, and rolled it over. It gathered speed and with arms and legs flailing as if wild, erratic life had been restored, slammed into a sapling, slithered round that to fall again and continue out of sight. Sounds of movement stopped. He was about to climb down to make certain it was as well concealed as possible, when he realised how dangerous it would be to leave traces next to the body – it was an axiom of crime detection that there was never contact without trace.

He picked up wallet, watch, gold ring, and clothes, crossed the clearing and began to climb. He came to an abrupt halt. The gun! He began to sweat, but not because of the heat. He was suffering the urge of a criminal to escape the scene of his crime, the panic that was every criminal's greatest enemy.

He returned to the clearing and picked up the gun, made certain the safety catch was on, searched for the empty cartridge cases. He thought he heard the sounds of someone approaching and tensed, ready to escape, but then realised that it had been a passing animal. Guilt turned molehills into mountain ranges.

As he waited by the road, making certain it was clear, he mentally tackled the problem. How to get rid of the Jaguar without causing trouble? To leave it in Port de Majerda must, sooner or later, raise the question of the whereabouts of the owner. Removing the engine, chassis, and number plates would make things more difficult in any investigation, but give cause to be certain there was reason for a thorough one. He had to make certain that when it was found, no one would bother about it. How? For the moment, no ready solution occurred to him.

There had been no sound of traffic for some time and a quick visual check showed the road to be clear in both directions – thank God for the fact that it led only up to the village! He left the cover and stepped on to the road and went round to the right-hand side of the Jaguar, realised his mistake and swore at his stupidity. He swore again when he found the doors were locked and he suffered the urge to run, to escape from the car which could incriminate him almost as quickly as the body . . . Self-control returned. He searched Doe's trousers and found the keys, pressed the central locking button and the locks clicked open. He dropped the bundle of clothes, wallet, gun, and ring, into the back well, settled behind the wheel. He'd make a very poor criminal unless practice really did make perfect.

He started the engine and drove off and as he turned the first corner, enjoyed a measure of relief, but only a small measure because before anything else, he had to get rid of the gun . . .

Handguns often failed to record fingerprints because butts were ridged and did not take impressions, but there were smooth surface which could, so he wiped the small automatic clean before he threw it, the empty cases, and the gold ring which bore no crest or other markings, into the centre of the river which ran down to meet the Mediterranean near Gransere.

Twenty-Seven

H e drove through Port de Majerda to the very wide front
road and parked on the central strip between a German
Audi and a Belgian Opel. He crossed to the kilometre-long
row of restaurants, cafés, ice cream parlours, memento shops,
banks, hairdressers, supermarkets, and travel agencies, and
went into a bank where he cashed all his remaining travellers'
cheques. Then he walked through the urbanizacíon to the
aparthotel, arriving hot and sweating. He explained to the
receptionist that he would not be using his room any more
since he'd met friends and would be staying with them. The
receptionist said he'd have to pay for the room that night
as it was now long after midday. He didn't argue, realised
that that was a mistake as he noted the scornful look on her
face. A Catalan, she would have argued interminably and she
would remember him because he hadn't.

He returned to the car and drove out to the slip road that
provided access to the autoroute which ran through to the
border. The *guardia* in the control post waved him through
without bothering to look at his passport which he held up;
there was no one visible in the French post. It seemed there
was one advantage to belonging to the European Union. At
the small bureau de change, he swapped all his pesetas for
francs. Cash seldom left a trail.

As he drove at a steady 110 kph – give the police no cause
to stop him – along the A9 autoroute, he tried to work out what

204

to do if Vaillant was not still dealing in stolen cars in Nevigny; failing to think up a feasible alternative to his present plan, he was left to hope that Vaillant had remained successful – an ironic hope by any policeman's standards.

Soon after midnight, he stopped in one of the rest lay-bys and slept fitfully for a couple of hours; before he left, he dropped Doe's shirt into one of the litter bins, shoes into another.

At eight in the morning, he had breakfast in a service area and discovered the claim that the worst coffee in France was always better than the best coffee in England was mistaken – in addition the croissants were stale. He left Doe's trousers in one litter bin, the empty wallet and pants in another.

He arrived in Nevigny in the middle of the afternoon. A large village or small town, depending on definitions, it possessed little of note beyond the church – not in itself in any way remarkable – in which hung a panel of needlework that was contemporary with the Bayeux Tapestry and, according to tradition, had been fashioned by the wife and three daughters of one of the Norman knights who had been killed as the Anglo-Saxon ranks broke.

The garage was on the outskirts; there was an office block, a showroom in which was a Renault which optimistically carried the sign 'Bargain', and a long shed, the bricks of which had been stained by time, oil, and muck. It was the kind of dated, agricultural garage where bangers were brought in the hopes that crude repairs could keep them running a little longer.

Ballard entered the office and the woman, young and pertly attractive, the only occupant, regarded him with supercilious uninterest, reminding him that he was unshaven and his clothes were rumpled. In as much French as he could muster, he asked if M. Vaillant was present; speaking very quickly, she replied she couldn't understand him. Certain she had, but was asserting every French person's determination to find foreigners' speech incomprehensible, he picked up a pencil from the desk and wrote down the name. She stared at this for so long that he became convinced Vaillant no longer owned the business and was probably in jail, when she said something that sounded impolite, stood, and walked out of the office, moving her buttocks with what she believed to be sinuous grace.

When she returned, she was accompanied by Vaillant. Short, tubby, balding, with hooded eyes, he was not a man from whom one would cheerfully buy a secondhand car. He stared at Ballard, made no attempt to speak.

"Monsieur Vaillant?"

He nodded.

"Do you understand English?" Ballard asked in French.

He shrugged his shoulders.

Ballard reverted to English. "I've been given your name."

Vaillant picked his teeth with a fingernail, then jerked his head as an indication to follow him. He left the office and crossed the small yard, littered with rubbish, into the shed. There were three cars inside, all ancient, all in varying stages of disassembly. He leaned against a workbench littered with engine pieces, brought a pack of Gitanes out of the pocket of his filthy overalls, lit a cigarette. "What you want?"

It had taken time, but Ballard had finally remembered the name of the man who had organised the theft of luxury cars in the UK and had then shipped them across to the Continent. "Charles said you'd be interested in what I've got for sale."

"Charles?"

"Roller Charles." A nickname earned by specialising in the top end of the luxury market.

Vaillant might not have heard.

"I've a Jaguar, less than a year old, left-hand drive, unmarked."

He drew on the cigarette, let the smoke trickle out of his nostrils.

"It's worth more than a hundred and fifty thousand francs to you. I'll take a hundred thousand."

Vaillant hawked and spat.

There was a long silence.

"How about ninety thousand for a quick handshake?"

"Bring in 'ere."

Ballard crossed the yard to the road and went along to the parked Jaguar. He drove into the yard, slowly in order to avoid the many obstacles, turned off the engine, climbed out. "You won't find a better one outside the showrooms."

Vaillant walked slowly around the car, opening each door in turn and examining the interior; he released the bonnet catch and propped up the bonnet to examine the engine. He sat behind the wheel, started the engine, revved fiercely; he drove forward so that the wheels straddled an inspection pit and used a spotlight to check the underneath of the car. When he came up out of the pit, he put the spotlight on a work bench and unplugged the long lead. "Papers?"

"There aren't any."

"Ten thousand francs."

"Are you laughing? It's nearly new." The genuine seller of a stolen car would haggle for every last penny, franc, peseta, or Deutschmark, so Ballard said that for a quick sale he'd take eighty thousand, but nothing less. Ten minutes later, they agreed fifteen thousand francs.

He was paid in crumpled, high-denomination notes. He asked to be driven to Calais and was charged a thousand francs, despite his angry accusations of highway robbery.

In Calais, there was a collecting box in aid of a cancer charity and he dropped the remaining fourteen thousand francs in this.

*　　*　　*

The first person Ballard met in the car park of divisional HQ was Frost.

"You've finally honoured us with your presence!" Frost said, with weary sarcasm.

"Couldn't bear to stay away any longer, Sarge."

"You don't look like you've been ill. More like you've seen some sun."

"An optical delusion. I've suffered some kind of flu."

"Some kind of flu! In my day, you had to be knocking at death's door before you took time off, now it's a couple of sneezes and you have to be tucked up in bed."

"The decline and fall of the British Empire."

"The likes of you don't have any way to fall. Leave the sick chit on my desk. There's a load of stuff down in the property room that needs logging. A Division wants a witness statement so tell Sam you'll be getting that and he can cover the Rawlings job." As Frost walked towards his car, he shouted out: "Don't forget the chit."

When there was no chit, there'd be trouble. But very minor trouble when compared with all the other problems which surrounded him. He was about to face Lock and had seldom ever wanted to do anything less . . .

He took the lift to the fourth floor, went along to the general room. Turner was the only person present. "Casanova returns!" He was in his most boisterous mood. "And from the look of things, you've had a heavy time."

"You could say that."

"So life's been one long hump?"

"Not quite."

"What's been the trouble? Couldn't enjoy yourself properly because you kept thinking what a naughty boy you were being?"

"Part of the time, it was like that."

"Blokes like you don't deserve the chances."

"Did you speak to Fleur for me?"

"She phoned here before I could get around to phoning her."

"What did she say?"

"Where were you? I said, on special operations and the fate of the country rested on your shoulders. She said you were working far too hard. I told her, you like things hard." He roared with laughter.

Ballard left the general room and went along the corridor. The door of the detective inspector's room was shut. He knocked, hoping there'd be no answer. He was a coward.

"Yes?"

Although not sunny, the day was muggy and Lock had taken off his coat and was sitting at his desk in shirtsleeves.

"Are you better?" he asked curtly.

"I haven't been ill."

He leaned back in the chair. "Then where in the hell have you been for the past few days?"

"Port de Majerda."

There was a silence.

"Why did you go there?" Lock finally asked.

"I discovered you received telephone calls from someone who lives there."

"How did you learn this?"

Ballard, bitterly conscious he was speaking to the husband he had cuckolded, said: "That doesn't matter."

"Very well. Perhaps you'll now explain why you obviously think there's significance in the fact that I do occasionally talk to someone who lives there?"

"It suggests that the long arm of coincidence has been stretched beyond breaking point."

"And your journey was intended to find out if this is so?"

"Yes."

"Did you succeed?"

"I discovered you are a traitor."

"You say that very dramatically!"

"Is that so surprising? Can't you understand what it means to me, never mind the force? When it first occurred to me that maybe it was you who'd done everything possible to scramble Aldridge's memory, I laughed the suggestion out of my mind. You were totally honest and incorruptible; all the time there were people like you in the police force, justice must survive. Then there was reason to suppose the suggestion might not be so ridiculous after all and although I hoped to hell I was making a bloody fool of myself, I had to check out things . . ."

"Why?"

"You can ask? If someone in your position is crooked, there can't be any guarantee of justice; if there's no justice, the whole of democratic life is threatened."

"You sound rather like an idealistic undergraduate."

"Idealism is to be sneered at?"

"To be examined carefully, rather than being accepted unquestioningly. Dishonesty is a concept, not an immutable fact; concepts change as circumstances change."

"Are you trying to argue you are not a traitor?"

"I'm asking if you can be so certain you know what is right and what is wrong."

"Yes."

"You won't accept that what is wrong today may be right tomorrow?"

"No."

"How do you judge a starving man who takes a loaf of bread from someone with more bread than he can eat?"

"He's a thief."

"A cruel verdict, surely?"

"The circumstances mitigate his guilt, not militate against it."

210

"Would you, then, arrest this man, however much your sympathy for him, and hope the court would hold that the circumstances should prevent his being punished?"

"Yes."

"That's known as passing the buck."

"As a policeman, it's my duty to carry out the law. It's the courts who decide judgements."

"From what you're saying, I imagine you intend to report your suspicions concerning me to county HQ?"

"Yes."

"And you'll be satisfied you're doing your duty?"

"If you like to put it in those terms."

"Do you always do your duty, no matter what?"

"I try to."

"You don't look at the possible consequences before you make the decisions?"

"If I did, I wouldn't be doing my duty."

"A man of total and absolute rectitude!"

"You can sneer."

"Not sneer, Ballard, admire your determination while regretting your lack of understanding of the human predicament . . . Have you stopped to wonder why I might betray my work and myself?"

"No."

"Because cause doesn't interest you, only result? But since all judgements need to be softened by compassion, I'm going to tell you why I did what I did."

"I don't think . . ."

"I don't give a damn what you think. You're going to listen, as much for your sake as mine." Lock pushed back his chair and stood, crossed to the window and looked down at the street below. "My wife, as do most women, wanted children, but for quite a while there was no luck. Then she had Lucy. It was a very difficult birth resulting in physical

211

damage that, the gynae man said, meant she couldn't have any more. It was a nasty blow, softened by Lucy. We were a very happy family."

After a long pause, Lock turned round. "Soon after she was six, she began to complain of headaches." He crossed to his chair and sat, leaned back and stared with unfocused eyes at the far wall. "All the usual tests proved negative, but the headaches became more frequent and intense and we consulted a specialist in London. He ordered more tests, causing Lucy great distress; my wife suffered the increasing fear that something really serious was wrong . . ." His expression tightened, his voice hardened. "Eventually, her fears were confirmed. Lucy had a tumour, deep within the brain and considered inoperable.

"Anyone who has not suffered a similar tragedy can only try to imagine the parents' horror, anger, despair. For us, it was a slow trip into hell. They said she might live another six months at best; immediate death would have been as much relief as tragedy for her and for us. In such a situation, life goes on, but one can't understand why.

"Then my wife read that a surgeon in Massachusetts had developed a radically new operation for this form of tumour and performed it on three patients, two successfully, one unsuccessfully. Had the odds been ninety-nine to one against, we'd still have seen this as a chance that had to be taken. We spoke to the specialist Lucy had been seeing and asked who in England could carry out the operation. He was a caring man, as sympathetic as a person in his job can afford to be, but he seemed to see no reason for shame in telling us that the British medical authorities considered the operation to be too radical to be undertaken until it had been further evaluated. He couldn't agree that it didn't matter how radical it was if Lucy was doomed to die within six months should nothing be done. That was that. Obviously, we then explored the alternative – taking Lucy to the States for the operation. When all the costs involved were evaluated, it became all too obvious there was no financial possibility of our being able to do this.

"I have a friend who works for the *Staple Cross Gazette* and one evening, after a few drinks, I poured my heart out to him. Without any reference to me, he wrote an article about Lucy and said the paper was setting up a fund to raise the money to send her to America for the operation. My wife called it a miracle. The chief constable called it something else. He hauled me up to county HQ and said Lucy could not benefit from any fund raised by the public because it could be thought that those who subscribed to it were trying to buy favourable treatment from the police . . . God knows, I argued with him, in terms that few chief constables would allow, but basically he's a decent, humane man and he didn't take offence. Or change his decision.

"When I told my wife, she crumpled . . ." He became silent.

"I don't see how all this is important," Ballard said, made uncomfortable by listening to another's tragedy.

"Because you're too convinced you know all the answers, too bloody certain you're morally right. The following week, the newspaper printed a brief note that the fund had been closed – no reason was given; most people must have assumed it had been set up too late and Lucy had died – and all those donors who could be identified would have their gifts returned, whilst any money not sourced would be handed to charity. I doubt anyone can even begin to imagine our feelings at seeing money freely given, money that might have saved Lucy, being returned to the givers.

"My wife became so depressed that she no longer bothered about the house or herself, only Lucy who was becoming weaker every day. Then there was a phone call. How much was needed to send Lucy and my wife to Boston and to have the operation performed? Between eighty and a hundred thousand pounds, I told the man. He said it was mine if . . . if I passed on certain information."

"A bribe. And you accepted it."

"No, Ballard, I didn't accept. I refused. But then I made the mistake of telling my wife what had happened. She demanded to know how I could place a sense of honour above my daughter's life. I tried to explain it wasn't like that, but she wouldn't, couldn't understand.

"There was a second phone call a few days later. Had I changed my mind? I replied I hadn't. My wife discovered this and put me on a mental rack with her accusations, pleas, despair, even hatred . . .

"One can only take so much. Three days and three phone calls later, I agreed to give the caller, who of course was Hastings, the information he wanted. He told me the money was in Switzerland and would be forwarded in the name of 'An anonymous benefactor'. Which is what happened. My friend on the *Gazette* printed an article extolling this act of generosity. The chief constable tried to object, but the fact that the donor was anonymous cut the ground from under his argument.

"Lucy and my wife flew to Massachusetts. Lucy was operated on and died three days later. By the time my wife returned home, she had convinced herself that had the operation been performed when first I was offered the money, Lucy would have survived. I was responsible for her death. Life at home continued to be hell."

"Then your treachery gained nothing."

"No doubt that pleases your sense of moral justice. The righteous like to see the sinners suffer because it heightens their righteousness. But in an odd way, my treachery – as you insist on terming it — has done some good. Both Jenner and Cairns have been killed . . ."

"Cairns is dead?"

"Blown to bits, along with two others."

"Are you trying to say that that justifies your actions?"

"If the word 'justify' offends you, I'll call the two events an unexpected bonus."

"Murder can be a bonus?"

"I have seen youngsters killing themselves or selling their bodies because they have become drug addicts. Anything which helps to prevent others following suit is a bonus."

"Hastings is as guilty."

"Probably more so."

"You accepted his bribe, which means you benefited from the degradation of those you profess to feel so sorry for."

"I took the money to save the life of my daughter, not because I was indifferent to the fate of other fathers' daughters . . . You need to learn that few, if any, are either wholly black or wholly white, or even consistently one or the other. Hastings deserves to die because of the tragedies he's brought to others. But as evil as he is, he possesses a sense of honour. When I gave him the information he wanted, he promised me that that was the end of the matter. Naturally I expected him to return with more requests and the threat of blackmail if I didn't accede to them. But there was no further demand, and as time passed, I realised that here was a man who could make foul money, yet honour his word. Then I did hear from him again. He asked me to do something to prevent the identification of those in the car which had accidentally killed Simon Kerr. He apologised for asking, made it clear that I must agree, then swore that whatever the future, this would be the last I'd ever hear from him . . . I don't suppose you can understand that there's a dichotomy in every man's sense of honour, justice, humanity?"

"No, I can't."

"A pity. It would help you to a more rounded understanding of the contradictions called life . . . Anyway, I did what I did. Then you started to upset things. Proving, as you did so, that if ever you can learn to regard yourself as no better than the next man, you will make a good detective. Too good by your own standards, since in part you are responsible for Cairns's murder."

"That's balls!"

"The truth often seems just that; most of us prefer to live in a world of hopeful imagination . . . When you raised the possibility that Cairns's car was the one which had run down the Kerr boy, you placed Cairns in danger. An efficient man of limited intelligence, he could see only one way of removing that danger – to get rid of you. The attempt failed. Hastings decided Cairns had to be killed because he saw the attempt as breaking his word to me – even if it had been you who was the intended victim. I don't doubt that he also feared Cairns was about to try to take over the mob . . . So perhaps now you can appreciate how your innocence has played a guilty part?"

"No," he replied hoarsely. His guilt was very clear in his own mind – but Lock knew nothing about the circumstances surrounding Doe's death. "And wrong can never be excused because of outside pressure – to allow that it can be is to justify any crime, even genocide when ordered by a superior."

"One should sacrifice oneself rather than carry out that order?"

"If necessary."

"You wouldn't accept that that's very easy to say, very difficult to do?"

"Not if one has standards."

"From this, do I take it you still intend to make a full report to county HQ?"

"Yes."

216

"You're a man of unusually strong character. Many of us have principles, very few are ready to honour them at no matter what cost to ourselves."

"Cost?"

"You haven't understood all the consequences? At the risk of boring you, I'll detail a little more of my personal affairs. My wife gradually succeeded in coming to terms with the death of Lucy, but never lost her belief that I was in large part responsible for our daughter's death. She saw my initial refusals to accept the bribe money as a betrayal of our daughter, so in an act of revenge she determined to betray me, by committing adultery with someone in the force. I tried to make her see how ridiculous this was. I suggested we saw marriage counsellors, psychiatrists, anyone who could help. She didn't want to be helped, she wanted revenge. So whenever there was the opportunity, she tried to seduce a member of CID. Only recently has she succeeded. And it was because Hastings phoned you when you were in bed with her . . ."

"That's ridiculous!" Even as she spoke, Ballard accepted the stupidity of trying to deny the fact.

"When I returned home from the symposium at county HQ, my wife told me what had happened because, long before, all sense of triumph had vanished and only guilty despair remained, as you will have gathered when you returned to the house in the morning – or are you so self-centred you were puzzled at her distress because you'd expected her to welcome you? Without becoming embarrassingly sentimental, I can say that our love for each other is sufficiently strong, because it has been tried by time, for us to be able to understand and accept things as they are and not vainly yearn for what might have been. It is to be hoped your fiancée will be able to understand and accept, since the truth of your betrayal of her must surface in the inquiry if you make your report to HQ."

"Are you trying to blackmail me into silence?"

"All I'm doing is to point out the inevitable result of your present refusal to accept that circumstances can alter the nature of events. But should you, on reflection, come to the conclusion that perhaps they do, it may interest you to know that I will soon be resigning from the force to join a private security firm who have been trying to persuade me to work for them for some time."

Ballard stared at Lock for an unaccountable time, then left. In a mental daze, he walked past the CID general room and went in the lift down to the ground floor, then continued outside into the sunlight which seemed so inapposite when his mind was in the black of midnight . . . If an inquiry was held, his actions concerning and following the death of Doe might well come to light – if they did, would the Spanish authorities demand extradition so that they could try him – that was, when they could find the time to do so? But of far more immediate concern was Fleur's reactions to learning about his one-night stand. Could she appreciate that his love for her had not been lessened by sex with Karen? Could she ever accept his betrayal when she believed loyalty in human relations to be the supreme virtue? He didn't know the answers, but was going to have to find out what they were. 'His honour rooted in dishonour stood, And faith unfaithful kept him falsely true.'

When he arrived at Ash Farm, Fleur raced around the corner of the house to meet him at the gate; she kissed him with open passion. Clutching him tightly, she said: "I've been so scared something terrible had happened to you when I never heard anything after Sam's call. I've been imagining all sorts of disasters." She kissed him again.

Her dark brown eyes were fixed on his with an intensity that said far more than her words. Because her love was so complete, his confession must be all the more devastating.

"Let's hurry indoors," she said as she stepped back and took hold of his hand. "When you rang to say you were coming here, Father wondered if your return should be marked by a bottle of champagne; needless to say, Mother and I were in agreement that there couldn't be any doubt. So now he's champing at the bit to pull the cork."

As they walked around the corner of the house, he remembered the book detailing how to enjoy a successful marriage on which it seemed she placed considerable store. Small wonder the author had suffered a divorce! Truth at all times was not the key to such success – occasionally, as he suddenly and unwillingly accepted, silence or a lie was far more relevant.